'... ... ... Leave

My Son Alone.

"I won't have you marrying him for his money."

Marnie swung around; spots of red in each cheek had replaced her pallor. "Please, you're blowing this all out of proportion. You don't know a thing about me!"

"The hell I don't. I know everything there is to know about you. Remember, I own this place."

"All this because your son took me out a few times?"

"We both know it's more than that." Tate O'Brien's voice cracked like a whip. "How much, Ms. Lee? How much will it take to make you leave my son alone?"

"How dare you!" Marnie cried, raising her hand with every intention of slapping his face. Tate was too quick; he caught her wrist in midair.

They glared at each other in silent rage. Neither was aware of the sights and sounds around them. Sunlight flooded the room. In the distance, a door slammed shut.

"Oh, why the hell not?" Tate muttered, then reached out, jerked her roughly to him and ground his lips against hers.

Dear Reader:

Welcome to Silhouette Desire—sensual, compelling, believable love stories written by and for today's woman. When you open the pages of a Silhouette Desire, you open yourself up to a whole new world—a world of promising passion and endless love.

Each and every Silhouette Desire is a wonderful love story that is both sensuous *and* emotional. You're with the hero and heroine each and every step of the way—from their first meeting, to their first kiss . . . to their happy ending. You'll experience all the deep joys—and occasional tribulations—of falling in love.

In future months, look for Silhouette Desire novels from some of your favorite authors, such as Annette Broadrick, Dixie Browning, Kathleen Korbel and Lass Small, just to name a few.

So go wild with Desire. You'll be glad you did!

Lucia Macro
Senior Editor

MARY LYNN BAXTER

SLOW BURN

SILHOUETTE *Desire*

Published by Silhouette Books New York

America's Publisher of Contemporary Romance

SILHOUETTE BOOKS
300 East 42nd St., New York, N.Y. 10017

ISBN: 0-373-05571-4

First Silhouette Books printing June 1990

Printed in the U.S.A.

MARY LYNN BAXTER

sold hundreds of romances before she ever wrote one. The D & B Bookstore, right on the main drag in Lufkin, Texas, is her home as well as the store she owns and manages. She and her husband, Leonard, garden in their spare time. Around 5:00 p.m. every evening they can be found picking butter beans on their small farm just outside of town.

One

____

Marnie Lee heard the commotion behind her and turned her head around.

Although Spencer's Place, an exclusive restaurant in west Houston, was crowded, she had no trouble figuring out why. A woman commanded the center of attention. Several persons were gathered around her. Then they seemed to back away, leaving the woman standing alone center stage.

Marnie gasped. Directly in her line of vision was Joan Collins, the superstar of the television show *Dynasty*.

Marnie's companion, Lance O'Brien, chuckled, effectively drawing her gaze back to him.

"I take it you're impressed," he said, laughter still in his voice.

Marnie knew he was making fun of her, but she didn't care. After all, how often did one get to see Joan Collins?

"Of course, I'm impressed," she said, smiling, "and so are you, only you won't admit it."

"Well," he drawled, easing back in his chair, his green eyes twinkling, "now that you mention it, she is a looker."

Following her acclaimed entry, the celebrity, a dazzling smile on her face, began moving toward Marnie and Lance's table. For a moment they watched her in action, spellbound. It was only after she was seated at a table by the window and batting her eyes at both her escort and the maitre d' that they turned away.

"I'm in shock," Marnie said. "I had no idea stars ate here."

"I take it you like the places I choose?"

Marnie's eyes sparkled. "That goes without saying."

Exclusive, classy restaurants, however, were just one of the amenities that Marnie had enjoyed since she'd been dating her boss, Lance.

From under the thick screen of her lashes, Marnie studied him, wondering again why she couldn't fall in love with him. She had concluded some time ago that the fault lay with her, because there was certainly nothing wrong with Lance, at least not as far as his appearance was concerned.

Not only was he good-looking and charming, he was the only son and heir of Tate O'Brien, who controlled Tate Enterprises and who seemingly had the power to turn sawdust into money.

So what if Lance's mouth and chin showed a definite weakness? Those flaws had been overlooked by a number of women; Lance had a reputation for being a heartbreaker.

Suddenly Lance chuckled, breaking her train of thought. "Wishing, huh?"

"Of course," Marnie said. "What woman doesn't wish she looked like her?"

"As far as I'm concerned, you look better."

At age thirty, Marnie could pass for twenty. She was tall and slender and moved with the grace of a dancer. Short, naturally curly light brown hair surrounded a heart-shaped face. Eyes like enormous black velvet pansies looked from under long lashes. When one first saw her, the words *remote* and *glorious* came to mind.

Marnie smiled. "We both know you're exaggerating, but it's nice to hear anyway."

Before Lance could comment further, the waiter seemed to appear from out of nowhere. Smiling politely at Lance, he asked, "Are you ready to order, sir?"

Lance turned to Marnie and raised his eyebrows inquiringly. "Same thing?"

"Same thing."

Having been to Spencer's Place with Lance on two other occasions, Marnie always ordered the house specialty—the Crabmeat Lorenzo. It was delicious, but then so was everything else on the menu.

While Lance discussed an appropriate wine with the waiter, Marnie's gaze wandered around the room. The mood in the front dining room, where they were sitting amidst a subtle decor and gleaming crystal, contrasted sharply with the middle room and colorful bar that sported bawdy paintings of nude ladies.

"What are you thinking about now?"

Once again swinging her attention back to Lance, Marnie smiled. "Actually, I was thinking how nice it is here and how much I'm enjoying myself."

"Yeah, it is kinda nice to relax after this week. God, it was a bitch."

A tiny frown blemished Marnie's forehead. "I couldn't agree more. It's been a long time since I've worked that hard."

But she didn't mind. In fact, hard work was her bailiwick, having recently been promoted to the engineering department where she was now an assistant on a special project.

Lance pushed a loose strand of brown hair from his forehead, then grinned. "Me, too. If this project won't make the old man happy, I don't know what will."

"I presume you're referring to your father."

Lance's grin was no longer in evidence. "One in the same, though I'm sure he wouldn't appreciate being called an old man." He suddenly grinned again, as if picturing Tate's reaction to his statement.

"I'm sure you're right," Marnie said, though she had never met the widowed Tate O'Brien. Rumors regularly floated around the office, hailing the big boss as more of a womanizer than his son.

Lance sighed. "I know I'm right. My dad doesn't tolerate imperfections in himself or anyone else, especially me."

"Well, as you say, he's bound to be pleased with the work you're doing on this project." Marnie's tone was light. "After all, you took his idea and made it work. Now we've got a government contract."

Though Lance's features brightened, his tone was cautious. "Yeah, who'd have thought Texas Systems would be asked to experiment with another type of plastic explosive?" He shook his head. "It's amazing."

"But exciting." Marnie shifted in her chair, oblivious to the clanking of silverware and glasses around her. "I've never worked on anything that's top secret before."

"Neither have I. Just hope we can give Uncle Sam what he wants."

"We will," Marnie said with confidence. "This project is going to put us on the map. You just wait and see."

"All I'm hoping for at the moment is to simply pull it off so that dad will get off my back."

It was a known fact that Tate was eager for his only son to eventually take over his entire business conglomerate, so that Tate could retire to his ranch and raise quarter horses. In order for Lance to learn the business from the ground up, he was being shifted from one company to the other, one department to the next.

"Don't worry, you'll do fine," Marnie said softly.

Instead of responding, Lance looked on as the waiter poured the wine. After sampling it, he murmured, "Mmm, perfect."

Once the waiter had disappeared again, Marnie reached for her glass and raised it to her lips. "You're right. It is delicious."

"Could you get used to this?" Lance asked, taking a slender hand in his.

Marnie slowly lowered her glass back to the table. "What do you mean?" Her tone was hesitant.

"You know what I mean."

Marnie shook her head as she carefully withdrew her hand. "No, I'm afraid I don't."

"Gonna make me spell it out, huh?"

"Guess you'll have to," Marnie said lightly.

Lance leaned back and stared at her with serious eyes. "What I'm saying is that you . . . we could dine like this every night—"

Marnie laughed, interrupting him. "You might could, but not me. Remember, I have to work for a living."

"You wouldn't if you married me."

Marnie's jaw went slack. "Excuse me."

"You heard what I said."

"You're . . . you can't be serious."

"Oh, I'm serious, all right. I've never been more serious."

Marnie blurted the first thing that came to mind. "But . . . but you're younger than I am."

Lance laughed. "Three years. Big deal. So, will you marry me?"

Marnie's heart sank. She shouldn't have been shocked by his impulsiveness, but she was. And flattered. No doubt about it, Lance O'Brien would be considered quite a catch. He had it all—looks, money, prestige and charm. However, Marnie had no intention of falling victim to that charm, especially now that her life held such promise.

But things had not always been this satisfying for Marnie, far from it, in fact. After having worked her way through college because her widowed father made very little money at his job in a small East Texas town, Marnie had been certain she was destined for great things, only to suddenly learn that her father had Alzheimer's disease.

Immediately Marnie had scrapped her own plans, making Silas Lee's well-being top priority. Though the following years had been riddled with hardship and pain, she didn't regret them. What she did regret was having to finally put her father in a special home.

While she missed him terribly, her highly challenging and rewarding work had been her salvation. It had taken the edge off her grief and had bolstered her confidence and given her financial security.

It was her new-found independence she treasured the most and guarded fiercely, refusing to take to heart any man's advances, especially those of Lance O'Brien.

"Well?"

Just as Marnie groped for something to say, the waiter arrived with their dinner. A sense of relief surged through her.

Once the waiter had departed, the silence continued as each concentrated on the entrées. However, the crabmeat tasted like a mouthful of paste in Marnie's mouth. It was useless; she couldn't pretend Lance's unorthodox proposal hadn't unnerved her.

The more she ate, the worse the food tasted. Finally, after eating at least half of it, she gave up and laid her fork down, then reached for her wineglass. Over the rim, she noticed Lance watching her. He, too, seemed uninterested in his food, though he'd managed to eat more than she had.

"Perhaps you'd care for a dessert," the waiter asked, suddenly appearing out of nowhere.

Marnie shook her head: "No thank you."

"Me neither," Lance said.

It was only after the tantalizing aroma of coffee drifted from the fine china cups that Lance spoke again.

"Well?" he repeated.

In spite of the seriousness of the situation, Marnie smiled. "Well, what?"

He again reached for her hand and squeezed it. "This is no game, Marnie."

"Do you make a habit of proposing to all the women you date?" she asked, forcing a lightness into her tone that she was far from feeling.

Lance's mouth formed a petulant slant. "I'm serious, Marnie. I'm in love with you and want to marry you."

Although Marnie did not take his proposal seriously, she nevertheless felt a trifle uncomfortable. Determination glinted in his eyes.

"You don't mean that, Lance."

"Yes, I do," he said stubbornly.

"You know I'm honored—"

"Dammit, Marnie, I don't want you to feel honored. I want you to say you'll marry me."

Marnie lifted her eyebrows. "I do believe you're serious."

"You're right, I am."

"Oh, Lance," she said, holding his gaze, "you know I've enjoyed seeing you these past months. But you also know that I've never pretended to be anything other than your friend."

"That can't change?"

"No, I'm sorry, but it can't. While I enjoy your company, I don't want to commit to anyone." Marnie's tone was gentle. "For the first time ever, I'm satisfied with my life. I want to enjoy my work and my freedom." She meant that, too. But even if it weren't the case, she was not in love with Lance O'Brien, nor could she ever be.

Lance leaned forward, that determined glint still in his eyes. "You're not going to get off the hook so easily. I'm warning you here and now, I'm not giving up."

"And I'm warning you that you're wasting your time."

Lance grinned, then stood. "Are you ready to party?"

"To party?" Marnie repeated, staring at him blankly.

"Yeah, my dad's throwing a shindig. We're gonna crash it, so I can introduce you."

Two

Marnie remained silent as Lance wheeled his Seville onto the blacktop road that led to the O'Brien ranch. She was loath to admit it, but her heart was pounding louder than usual.

While Lance had denied a second time that there was anything wrong with crashing his father's party, Marnie's doubts persisted. Even if Tate did not object, she did. Fraternizing with the rich and famous held no interest for her. Still, she was curious about the T Bar Ranch.

Not only had there been gossip pertaining to the man himself, but his private domain, as well. Supposedly it was a showplace, as on more than one occasion visiting heads of states had stayed there.

During the fifteen-mile trip, very little conversation had taken place between Lance and her. Several times she had looked at him, noticing each time that his jaw was set at a stubborn angle. Since they had left the restaurant, he hadn't said any more about the proposal.

But she feared he didn't intend to give up even though she felt certain he wasn't serious, despite what he said. As with the sundry other women in his life, she was just a passing fancy. When he realized she had no intention of sleeping with him, he'd cut her loose. Lance wanted a playmate; she wanted a soul mate.

She'd miss him; she couldn't deny that. Though spoiled and selfish on the one hand, on the other he was fun loving and eager to please. Still, as she'd told him, she didn't love him and knew she never would.

Now, seeing the lights from the house twinkling like stars through the thick foliage, she turned toward him.

"It's not too late to change your mind, you know."

Taking his eyes off the road, he returned her stare, a grin plastered across his handsome face. "Hey, come on, where's your sense of adventure? Anyway, Dad's not that bad. It's only when I'm around that he seems to take on a different personality."

"So what's the purpose of our coming here, then?"

Lance sighed with exasperation. "I told you I wanted you to meet him."

This time it was Marnie who sighed. "All right. Whatever you think best." Why argue with him, she thought. Actually, she was making far too big a deal of it. Tate O'Brien was no god.

Lance braked the car on the circular drive in front of the sprawling, brick house. Huge oak and pecan trees hovered over the structure, and Marnie had the feeling she had entered an enchanted forest. How lovely, she thought, entranced, watching as the moon spotlighted the poised elegance of the entryway.

"We won't stay long, I promise," Lance said.

Marnie's smile was skeptical. "Why is it that I don't trust you?"

"Because you're a distrusting female, that's why," Lance said, tweaking her on the nose.

Marnie rolled her eyes. "Let's go."

The instant she stepped into the fresh night air, the smell of honeysuckle caressed her senses. She paused and breathed deeply, reveling in the sweet scent. Close by, crickets chirped, while the wind whispered through the trees. The spring evening was perfect. If it was left up to her, she would sit in the swing on the porch and never take a step inside.

"Come on," Lance urged. "I want a drink."

When they reached the massive front door, Lance didn't bother to knock. Instead he thrust it open and with an innocent smile, indicated that Marnie should precede him. The instant she crossed the threshold into a large foyer, she came face-to-face with an overweight, stern-faced woman.

However, when she saw Lance, her lips spread into a wide grin.

"Lord a mercy, I was beginning to think you'd crawled off somewhere and died."

"And leave you," Lance responded heartily, "the best cook in the entire state of Texas? No way," he added, leaning over and giving her a kiss on the cheek.

"Then why haven't we seen more of you?" she demanded, blushing.

"Because I've been working, that's why."

The woman snorted.

Lance laughed, then turned to Marnie and reached for her hand. "Annie Bullock, meet Marnie Lee."

Marnie extended her hand and smiled warmly. "Hello, Annie."

"Hello ma'am."

"Annie's all things to all people in this household. In fact, without her, this place couldn't function."

"He likes to exaggerate," Annie said, leveling gray eyes on Marnie. "But it's nice to hear anyway."

"Where is everybody?" Lance asked, changing the subject. "On the deck?"

Marnie was wondering the same thing. Although she could hear soft music, clinking glass and muted laughter, she hadn't as yet seen anyone.

Annie cast her gaze sideways. "There and in the den."

"Grandmom, too?"

Annie's face lost some of its animation. "No. She called saying she didn't feel well."

"Mmm, hope it's nothing serious."

"I'm sure it isn't or your dad would've called off the party."

"Speaking of Dad," Lance said, cupping Marnie's elbow, "it's time we made our presence known."

Annie smiled. "Hope you'll come again, Marnie."

"Oh, she will," Lance said, urging her forward.

After giving Lance a dark look for answering for her, Marnie scanned her surroundings. The interior was breathtaking. To her right was a formal living room, its walls lined with what Marnie guessed were highly prized paintings. Beyond she could see a hallway that led to the bedrooms. On her left were the kitchen and formal dining room.

It was obvious that when this home was constructed and furnished, money was no object. It reeked with opulence.

"Well, what d'you think?" Lance asked, still holding her elbow.

"Need you ask?"

Lance chuckled. "Dad had it built a couple of years ago, right after he started grooming me to take over the business. Grandmom decorated it for him."

"Is she your dad's mother?"

"Yep. She's some lady, too. I'm sorry you won't get to meet her tonight."

"Me, too," Marnie said, just as she and Lance paused on the threshold of a magnificent room that spanned the back of the house.

"Want a glass of wine?" Lance asked, drawing her attention back to him.

She smiled. "Please."

"Don't move." Lance squeezed her elbow. "I'll be right back. Then we'll circulate."

A number of guests thronged the large deck, wandering in and out of the double doors thrown open to the warm spring night. There were clusters of people standing on the lawn, sharing drinks and animated conversation.

Marnie couldn't help but breathe a sigh of relief that she was appropriately dressed. Her long-sleeved turquoise silk jumpsuit and silver looped earrings blended in with the cocktail dresses, both long and short.

Focusing once again on the room itself, she perused the premises. But instead of taking in the rustic beams overhead or the huge fireplace, her gaze fell on a tall, broad-shouldered man with a mustache standing a few feet away.

A sudden and unexpected tingle climbed Marnie's spine. Even if he hadn't resembled his son, instinct would have told her that the man was Tate O'Brien. It wasn't so much the way he was dressed that set him apart, though his casual navy jacket, gray slacks and yellow shirt were certainly in contrast to his guests' formal attire. No, it was the man himself. Cool arrogance seemed to radiate from him. Here, she thought, was a man who was used to giving orders and having them obeyed.

Marnie tried to remove her gaze but found she could not. Blue eyes that burned like coals continued to hold her captive. There was something magnetic about him, as well, something larger than life that made her want to reach out to him. Such a thought was so ridiculous, it was terrifying. She felt herself turn pale.

Then, suddenly, he bent and said something to the stately blond woman at his side.

It was only after Tate straightened and began moving in her direction that Marnie panicked. Surely he wasn't going to seek her out? Of course, he was, she told herself. After all, she was a stranger. Logic told her that seeking her out was *exactly* what he would do.

Where was Lance? Frantic, she searched the crowded room.

"Missed me, huh?"

Lance's voice grazed her ear, and she went limp with relief. "Yes, as a matter of fact I did," she said, "only not for the reason you're thinking."

As if unaffected by her dry tone, Lance grinned and handed her a glass of wine. "What's up?"

"Your father. That's what's up. If I'm not mistaken, he's heading our way."

"So you didn't want to face dear ole dad alone." Lance leaned closer to her ear. "All you have to remember is that his bark's much worse than his bite."

Marnie gave him a dark look before Tate O'Brien once again consumed her vision. He had stopped within touching distance. Unconsciously, Marnie stepped back as the full impact of his rugged good looks struck her like a blow.

Like his son, Tate had the same wide forehead and high cheekbones. But there the resemblance ended. His hair was thick and dark with a spattering of white above each ear. His sensitive lower lip balanced by a resolute chin would have gone a long way toward making his face perfect had his expression not looked so grim.

"Hello, son."

"Hello, Dad," Lance said, placing an arm around Marnie's shoulders and pulling her against his side. "I'd like you to meet Marnie Lee."

As if it were foreign to his nature, Tate smiled, then nodded. "Ms. Lee. It's a pleasure."

But it wasn't, Marnie thought. He wasn't pleased; he wasn't pleased in the least. To her dismay she felt a flush stain her cheeks, his quick appraisal making her uncomfortable as well as contributing to the strained atmosphere. "Same here, Mr. O'Brien," she replied in her coolest tone.

"Have we met before?" he asked, a frown altering his brow.

Lance cut in. "Marnie works for Systems." He paused and winked at Marnie. "Actually, she's our new project assistant and works directly with me."

"I see," Tate said, giving Marnie another long look, a look that had an even more unsettling effect on her. It bore the stamp of cold hostility and wary distrust. For heaven's sake, who did he think she was—a gold digger out to trap his son?

Refusing to let him intimidate her, Marnie squared her shoulders and smiled.

"Surprised to see me...us, Dad?" Lance asked, changing the subject.

Focusing his attention back on his son, Tate said, "As a matter of fact, I am. So tell me, what do you want?"

Marnie almost gasped aloud at his rudeness.

Lance flushed. "What makes you think I want something?"

"That's the only time you ever come home, isn't it?"

"Well, this time you're right," Lance said flatly. "I wanted you to meet Marnie."

For the moment no one spoke. Forgotten were the laughter and cocktail conversations behind them. It was almost as if the three of them were alone in the room.

Tate was the first to break the heavy silence. "Ms. Lee, will you excuse us for a minute? I'd like to talk to Lance alone."

"Of course." Marnie couldn't think of anything she'd like more than to be rid of Tate's charismatic presence.

Lance turned to her. "Will you be all right?" he asked, his tone conveying concern.

Marnie nodded. "I'll be fine. You go ahead."

Tate's eyes sought hers, and she felt herself blush.

"Make yourself at home," he said. "Join in the party."

Disconcerted, she smiled lamely. "Thank you."

Although his deep, rich voice was polite and unemotional, Marnie was not fooled. Tate O'Brien did not like her. On the heels of that certainty came another: he would make a very formidable enemy.

Standing like a statue, she watched Lance and Tate disappear through a door adjacent to the bar. As if feeling her gaze on him, Tate turned. For the briefest of moments, their eyes met again and held. Then, turning, he closed the door behind him.

Marnie shuddered.

* * *

Tate's office had its own distinct personality. Here he could relax and, for a blessed moment, forget his work and the huge responsibilities that often mastered him.

The room, with its light walnut paneling, thick tan carpet, bookshelves lined with books, paintings of prized quarter horses and massive walnut desk, seemed to hold him. At this point in time, however, the room failed to render its soothing effect.

This evening he couldn't kid himself. He knew why. Nevertheless, the thought made him fiercely angry. Marnie Lee. She was the culprit; she was responsible for a fire burning in his gut.

Since Stephanie's death there had been many women. They had moved in and out of his life like a revolving door. Yet few had made an impression, certainly not a lasting one. And he had never said the word *love* to another woman, nor did he intend to.

So why had his reaction to Marnie been so quick, so intense? Granted, she was lovely.

Her hair, shining like spun gold, had framed her face; her generous breasts had filled the outfit she was wearing.

Still he'd had other women equally as beautiful, if not more so. But there was an innocent allure about her. She probably wasn't aware of it, but she was the kind of woman a man would throw a few punches to get to.

His son proved to be no exception.

Sighing deeply, Tate switched his attention to the muted sounds of laughter and clinking glass. If he

were to turn his head a tad, the deck would be in full
view. He knew it would be cluttered with guests taking advantage of the perfect weather.

The party was in full swing; his guests were having
a good time. But right now he wasn't concerned about
the success or failure of his party. He was concerned
about Lance and his relationship to Marnie Lee.

From behind him the sound of a sigh, deeper than
his own, forced him around.

"Don't you think you've stalled long enough?"
Lance seemed to be hanging on to his patience by a
thread. "Just say what's on your mind and be done
with it. Marnie'll be wondering what's happened to
me."

Lance was sitting in one of the leather chairs, arms
folded across his chest, legs sprawled straight out in
front of him. His features were pinched, effectively
depicting his surly attitude.

"Let her wonder," Tate said, his tone acid.

"What's that supposed to mean?"

Tate cleared his throat and returned his son's hos-
tile stare. The conversation was off to a bad start; he
had told himself he would use patience in dealing with
Lance, but lately, whenever they got together, patience flew out the window.

Lance again shattered the silence. "What the hell's
going on?"

"Calm down." Tate's order was withering.

Lance flushed. "I wish you'd stop treating me like
a kid, like I don't have enough sense to get in out of a

good hard rain. For chrissake, Dad, I'm twenty-seven years old.''

"Then bygod act like it.''

Lance lunged to his full height, his face blood-red. "Look, if all you brought me in here for is to argue, then forget it. I'm leaving.''

"Sit down.'' Tate's tone was cold and brooked no argument.

Lance's fury seemed almost palpable, but he sat down, albeit ungraciously.

"That's better,'' Tate said. Again, he knew he was going about this all wrong. He vowed to contain his anger.

"Okay, so what have I done wrong this time?'' Lance demanded. When Tate opened his mouth to answer, he went on, "I've been busting my ass on this special project, and up till now I thought everything was going okay.''

"It's not your work,'' Tate replied soberly. "At least not directly.''

Lance arched an eyebrow. "Ah, ha, I get it; you're steamed because I borrowed some money from Gran and haven't paid it back.''

"While that doesn't make me any too happy, that's not the reason I wanted to talk to you.'' Tate rocked forward for emphasis. "But now that you mentioned it, you sure as hell better pay her back.''

"So, if it's not Gran and it's not work . . .'' Lance's voice played out.

"Marnie Lee. It's Marnie Lee." Tate watched his son carefully, half expecting him to explode. Instead he looked dumbfounded and confused.

"Marnie? I don't get it."

"Oh, I think you get it, all right," Tate sneered. "In fact, I think you get the *complete* picture."

Lance's mouth tightened, but he didn't say anything.

"For god's sake, I'm not blind. I saw the way you looked at her."

"And *I* saw the way *you* looked at her!"

Tate's eyes narrowed dangerously. "Dammit, boy, watch your mouth."

"Sorry," Lance muttered, averting his eyes, as though he realized he had gone too far.

For another long moment neither spoke. They simply stared at each other, their harsh breathing the only sound in the room.

As if finally conceding defeat, Lance flopped back down into the chair. "So what about her?" he demanded. His tone was testy at best.

Tate hesitated and chose his words carefully. "I don't want you to see her anymore, that's what."

For a second time blood rushed into Lance's face. "Just why the hell not?"

"Because I don't want a replay of the last fling you had."

"Marnie's different."

Tate laughed without humor. "If I recall, that's what you said about Melissa."

"Well, we proved the baby wasn't mine, didn't we?" Lance wiped his brow. His discomfort was obvious.

"It could've been, though. Right?"

"You know the answer to that," Lance said petulantly.

"You damn right I do. That's the reason for this conversation right now. When are you going to learn you can't fall in love with every girl you meet and promise her the moon?"

"I told you, Marnie's different."

"I beg to differ with you." Tate's tone dripped with sarcasm. "True, she's better-looking than the others and seems to have a little more breeding, but that doesn't mean a damn in the scheme of things. I still don't want you involved with her."

"Is it because she works for the company?" Lance sounded a tad desperate.

"You haven't heard a word I've said, have you?" Tate asked, clearly frustrated.

Lance stood again and shoved his hands down into his pants pockets. "Yes, I have, but I told you, Marnie's different."

"Spare me. She's probably after your money, just like Melissa was and the others before her."

"No, she's not!"

"How do you know?"

"I just know."

"Do you know anything about her family, her friends?"

"I know enough."

Tate muttered a stream of epithets.

"Well, since you opened this can of worms," Lance said, "you might as well hear it all."

Tate tugged at his mustache. "Hear what?"

"I've asked Marnie to marry me."

"You what!"

Lance's chin jutted defiantly. "You heard me."

"Oh, for heaven's—" Tate began with suppressed violence, only to suddenly break off. With great effort he fought to control himself. He knew if he said anything else, he'd regret it.

"She's a warm, wonderful person, and I love her," Lance was saying.

"Love! You don't know the meaning of the word. When are you going to learn *lust* is not love."

"I'm sorry you feel that way, Dad," Lance said without emotion, "but I've made up my mind and there's nothing you can say or do to stop me."

With that Lance turned and walked out of the room, slamming the door behind him.

Tate had no idea how long he stood there in the middle of the room, his heart pounding like an out-of-shape runner climbing a steep hill. It was all he could do to keep from charging out the door and hauling his son back into the room.

And do what? he asked himself. Argue some more? Pound some sense into him? Hardly. He couldn't afford to add more fuel to fanned flames. Another expletive singed the air, but it didn't make him feel better. When had he and his son become adversaries instead of friends? he wondered. He could remember the time they used to be buddies, used to enjoy each other's company.

God knows, he loved him. Was Tate's mother right? Was he too overprotective? But then he had a good reason for doing so, only Lance didn't see it that way. Again Tate paused in his thoughts to rub the back of his neck, hoping to relieve some of the tension lodged there. It hadn't worked a little while ago, and it wasn't working now. His insides remained tightly knotted.

No way was he going to stand by and watch Lance ruin his life. He would find a way to stop his son from marrying Marnie Lee.

Suddenly he snapped his fingers, then reached for the phone. After punching out the numbers, he waited.

"Neal, O'Brien. I want you to run a second security check on someone. Pronto."

Three

———

"Well?"

"Well what?"

In the soft semidarkness Marnie searched Lance's features. "That innocent act won't work with me and you know it," Marnie retorted. She'd wanted to question him earlier, but common sense warned her to hold her tongue.

They were in the driveway of her condominium now, and she knew Lance hadn't gotten over his anger. Perhaps fury was a more appropriate word, Marnie thought, her gaze still on him. But instead of returning her scrutiny or answering her question, he continued to stare ahead in brooding silence.

In that moment he looked exactly as his father had looked after he'd walked out of his study, a thundercloud ready to erupt.

During the time they had been behind closed doors, Marnie had meandered around the room, sipping on her wine, only to eventually find herself out on the deck. Several couples she didn't know had spoken to her, while two men had approached her and asked if they could get her another drink. She had politely declined, her mind occupied with what was taking place behind closed doors.

It had been only moments after she'd wandered back inside the house that they had appeared. The instant Lance had spotted her, his face had lost its sullenness and he'd winked. Tate's, however, had remained granite hard. He hadn't even bothered to look her way.

Arrogant bastard, she'd thought then, and still did.

Finally breaking into the heavy silence, Marnie said, "I take it your conversation with your dad was not a pleasant one."

Lance's laugh was harsh. "That's putting it mildly."

"It was about me, wasn't it? Your disagreement, I mean."

Lance twisted slightly to face her. His lips were drawn into a fine line. "How'd you know?"

Marnie shrugged her slender shoulders. "Intuition, I guess."

"Well, you're right," Lance said flatly.

For some unexplainable reason, Marnie felt an instant's anxiousness in the pit of her stomach. Was it possible that her job might be in jeopardy?

Marnie's tone was hesitant. "Why was I discussed?"

"I told him I was going to marry you."

There was an instant of absolute silence.

Marnie's heart sank. "Oh, God, you didn't. Please tell me you didn't."

Lance's lips formed a pout. "I sure as hell did."

"You know, Lance," Marnie said with saccharine sweetness, "if I weren't afraid of being cooped up in a little room all day long and forced to sew, which I detest, I'd gladly strangle you."

An uncertain smile replaced the pout.

"It's not funny," Marnie snapped.

Lance scratched his ear and sighed. "No, I guess it isn't, but damn..." His voice faded.

A fiery glint lit Marnie's eyes. "You had your nerve, especially after I had made it quite plain that I had no intention of marrying you—or anyone else, for that matter."

"And I warned you I wasn't taking no for an answer."

"So what did he say?" Marnie asked, despising herself because she was curious. When Lance didn't respond, she continued. "He doesn't think I'm good enough for you, does he?" Even to herself, her voice sounded choked.

Lance shifted uneasily. "Don't take offense. He doesn't think anyone's good enough for me. He looks at me as one of his prized quarter horses."

"Maybe that's his way of showing you he cares," Marnie said.

"Yeah."

"I don't suppose you bothered to put his mind at rest by telling him that I'd declined your offer of marriage?"

Even though the darkness hampered her vision, she knew Lance's face turned red.

She turned away. "No, no I guess you didn't."

Suddenly feeling drained, and realizing this conversation was going nowhere, Marnie added, "Look, it's getting late. I should be in bed. Tomorrow, as you well know, is going to be another busy day."

Lance reached for her hand. "You aren't still mad at me, are you, honey?" His tone was cajoling.

"No, Lance, I'm not mad at you. I'm just furious."

He gave her a blank look, then laughed. "Good, that means I still have a chance to change your mind."

She opened her mouth to say something, only to snap it shut. Nothing she could say, she realized, would dent his thick skull. Shaking her head, she merely opened the door and stepped out. It was only after she'd let herself inside the condo and flipped on the entry-hall light that she heard him crank the car and drive off.

Closing her eyes, she sank against the door.

Marnie took a sip of the hot decaffeinated coffee and wiggled deeper into the plush cushions on the sofa. She was too keyed up to sleep, so she hadn't even bothered to go to bed.

Her shapely legs, covered by her flimsy robe, were resting on the glass-topped table in front of her. Feeling the hot liquid steal through her like a soothing balm, she smiled and closed her eyes.

But her feeling of contentment didn't last long. The events of the evening rose again to haunt her.

"Don't think about him," she hissed aloud. "Forget you ever met him."

That was a joke, she thought, curling her lip scornfully. How did one go about forgetting a specimen like Tate O'Brien? She certainly could not. While she had disliked him on sight, she had found him fascinating, as well. Maybe it was his rugged good looks that had commanded her interest. She'd often heard the statement that a man looked better as he grew older, while a woman looked worse. Where Tate was concerned, that was true. Office gossip had him at forty-five, fifteen years her senior. Yet, she'd bet he'd never looked better.

Furious with the mind games she was playing, Marnie took another gulp of the coffee only to suddenly cough, nearly choking on it.

"Damn," she muttered, slamming her cup down on the table beside her. Then, determined to get hold of her scattered emotions, she curled her feet under her and looked around.

No matter how low she was feeling, the sight of her lovely home almost always cheered her up.

The condo had six rooms: a living area with two skylights and a fireplace, a kitchen with an adorable breakfast nook, two bedrooms and two baths. With its traditional furnishings, it exuded warm, cozy comfort.

She had worked damn hard to get it, too. But then she'd had to work hard for everything she'd ever had. Lance hadn't, she reminded herself. That, along with the fact that she didn't love him, was exactly why marriage between them could never work.

Their life-styles differed, as well. Yet, she had nothing to be ashamed of. Though she was reared with no amenities, she was proud of her family and her upbringing. Most of all, she was proud of her accomplishments. And nothing or no one, she vowed, was going to undermine her success or her newfound contentment, least of all Tate O'Brien.

Suddenly feeling the need to cling to something familiar, her eyes strayed to the collection of pictures adorning her mantel. One stood out: a picture of her father dressed in overalls. A huge grin lit his face. Unwinding her legs, she got up and walked to it and with her index finger, traced the frame lovingly. Though she tried to blink them back, tears burned her eyes like fire.

Silas didn't even recognize her now, and that broke her heart. Still she would never forsake him. That was why this job meant so much to her. In addition to providing her with this condo, it allowed her to keep her father in that very expensive home.

Thoughts of Tate O'Brien once again flared in her mind, and her blood turned to ice water in her veins. Damn Lance and his proposal. If he caused her to lose her job...

A sob caught in her throat at the same time the doorbell rang. Startled, Marnie peered down at her watch. Eleven-thirty. Frowning, she crossed to the door and stared out the peep hole.

Then wide-eyed, she flung the heavy door open. "Why, Katie, what on earth brings you out this time of night?"

"Saw your light and thought you might offer this poor, tired soul a cup of decaf coffee."

Marnie grinned as her next-door neighbor and friend, Kate McCall, crossed the threshold. Dressed in a conservative blue flight attendant's uniform, she could have passed for a strict teacher in a private school if she hadn't smiled and shown her dimple.

"Don't tell me you just got home," Marnie exclaimed.

"From New York, no less."

Marnie laughed again. "Well have a seat and I'll take pity on you and pour you a cup of coffee."

Following her divorce a year ago, Kate had left her job at a computer company and gone to work for American Airlines. Like Marnie, she had been looking for a way to escape her grief. They had become firm friends.

Marnie saw the tired lines around Kate's eyes, and her heart went out to her.

"God, what a day," Kate said, collapsing on the couch.

"You look it, too." Even though Kate was just a year older than she, tonight she looked ten.

Kate feigned anger. "Thanks a heap, friend."

Smiling, Marnie disappeared into the kitchen. Moments later she returned with her cup refilled and another one brimming full for Kate.

"Well, let's hear about your day," Marnie said, sitting down on the opposite end of the couch, then handing Kate her cup.

Kate latched onto it with a sigh. "There's nothing to tell, really. Supervisors were on board, and everyone was chasing tail trying to please." She paused and blew on her coffee. "After we landed, several of us went out to dinner to celebrate their departure."

Marnie sighed. "I can sympathize. My day wasn't a whole lot better."

Kate raised her dark eyebrows. "Your day or your evening?"

"What made you ask that?"

Kate shrugged. "I don't know. There's just something not quite right about your eyes. You're worried about something, right?"

"You're much too nosey for your own good, Kate McCall." Marnie's smile took the sting out of her words.

Kate batted the air with her free hand. "Friends are supposed to be nosey," she countered, unperturbed.

"It isn't your father, is it?" Now there was an anxiousness to her tone.

"No...no, he's the same."

"Does it have anything to do with Lance?"

An affirmative nod was all Marnie was able to get in before Kate went on. "So, what happened?"

Without answering, Marnie leaned forward and adjusted the pillows behind her back.

Kate's blue eyes never wavered from her.

"How 'bout something to eat?" Marnie said suddenly, desperately, realizing how close she was to tears. And the last thing she wanted to do was cry in front of Kate. God, but Tate O'Brien had certainly done a number on her. Damn that man.

"Hey, you are upset. Didn't you just hear me tell you that I came straight here from the restaurant?" Kate frowned. "But in answer to your question, no I don't want anything to eat. What I do want is for you to confess. Furthermore, I'm not budging until you do."

"It's...Lance."

"He didn't dump you did he?"

"No, quite the contrary."

"Ah, ha." A slow, knowing grin spread across Kate's lips. "He asked you to marry him, I'll bet."

"Yes, he did," Marnie said quietly.

"Praise the Lord. I certainly hope you had the good sense to say yes."

Marnie blinked, then stared at her friend, her eyes enormous in her pale face. "Surely you aren't serious."

"Of course, I'm serious." Kate wrinkled her forehead and edged forward on the couch. "Why, Lance O'Brien is every woman's dream. Not only is he good-looking, but he has money to burn."

"But I don't love him, Katie," Marnie wailed.

"Pooh, that's not important."

Marnie struggled to hold on to her patience, knowing it was too late and she was too tired to be having this conversation. But short of telling Kate to mind her own business and go home, she had no choice but to hear her out.

"Well, it's important to me," Marnie said, her tone sober.

Kate bounded off the couch, then immediately peered down into Marnie's face, an incredulous expression on hers. "Why? I bet you can't answer that."

"Oh, come on, Kate, how can you ask a question like that? You know yourself that even with love, it's difficult to make a marriage work." Marnie paused and spread her hands, trying to get her point across to her friend. "Sometimes impossible, right?"

For a moment Kate averted her eyes, as if unable to meet Marnie's intent gaze. Then she faced her squarely and said, "Wrong. I didn't love Grant the way I should have going in, but that wasn't all that broke up our marriage. It was money," she added bluntly. "The lack of it."

Marnie sighed deeply and didn't say anything.

"Look, sweetie," Kate said, following the short silence, "you can tell me to go take a flying leap if you want to for interfering in your business—" she grinned lopsidedly "—but you know I care what happens to you."

"I know."

"I see how hard it is for you to keep your father in that special home, how hard you have to work."

"Oh, Katie, I know you care. And you're right, it is tough. But that doesn't mean that I should marry the first rich man who comes along. I couldn't be happy living that way."

"So I can only assume then that you're waiting for a hunk to walk up to you and sweep you off your feet?"

Suddenly Tate O'Brien's face again rose to the forefront of her mind. Mortified, Marnie turned away from Kate's probing stare, but not soon enough, she knew, to hide the color that surged into her face.

"So, I'm right," Kate said, chuckling. "That's exactly what you're waiting for."

Both relieved and thankful that Kate had misunderstood her discomfort, Marnie smiled. "Maybe...I don't know. But what I do know is that I could never fall in love with Lance O'Brien, even though he is a lot of fun."

"Well, I can understand that, especially after being closeted with your father for so long and never having time to play. And from what you've told me, Lance certainly knows how to show a woman a good time." Kate smiled without envy.

"Unfortunately it might not be *me* he shows a good time any longer."

Kate sat back down on the couch. "Because you turned down his proposal? He's upset, huh?"

"To tell you the truth, I'm not sure Lance has taken no for an answer."

Kate shook her head. "I don't get it. If that's the case, why won't you be seeing him anymore?"

Ignoring her, Marnie latched onto an errant strand of hair that grazed her cheekbone and toyed with it for a minute. Then, thrusting it behind her ear, she said, "It really doesn't matter about Lance because his father, Tate O'Brien, doesn't like me."

"So?"

"So if Lance wants to continue the life-style to which he's accustomed, he'll have no choice but to give in to his father's demands."

Kate was clearly puzzled. "He works, doesn't he?"

"Of course, he works. At the moment he's actually my boss. *However*—" Marnie stressed the word "—the salary he makes isn't enough. It's as simple as that."

"So dear ole dad doles it out for the right to control his life."

"That's it in a nutshell."

"So how do you know Daddy doesn't approve of you?" Kate pressed.

Marnie couldn't help but smile at the way Kate said "Daddy" as if it was some kind of contagious disease that should be avoided at all cost. "He thinks I'm a gold digger."

Kate slapped her neck and laughed out loud. "You've got to be kidding?"

"No, I'm not kidding," Marnie said, her lips now set in a taut line.

"Did he actually call you that to your face?"

"No, but I could read it in his eyes." Suddenly seeing the lack of understanding on Kate's face, Marnie told her all about the party. What she didn't tell her friend was her volatile reaction to Tate.

"Wow," Kate said when Marnie finished.

"So you think your job could really be in danger?"

Marnie suppressed a sigh. "I hope not, but you never know."

"So are you going to humor 'Daddy' and stop seeing Lance?"

For the first time in a long while, Marnie's eyes lit up. "Probably not."

Kate grinned. "Atta girl. And if 'Daddy' pulls anything underhanded, you can slap him with a harassment suit."

"Sure thing," Marnie said drolly.

Still grinning, Kate stood. "Well, I gotta go. As it is, I've overstayed my welcome. In the morning I wouldn't blame you if you came looking for me with a shotgun."

"When that alarm goes off at five o'clock, I may very well do that."

Kate leaned over and gave Marnie a quick bear hug. "Good night, and thanks for the coffee. Talk to you later."

Marnie returned the hug. "I'll keep you posted on what happens."

"That goes without saying," Kate called over her shoulder, letting herself out the door.

Marnie heard him before she saw him.

She had only minutes before entered Lance's office, having brought with her important paperwork on the project that had to be completed before noon. She'd needed absolute quiet, and since Lance was out of town, she'd opted to use his office.

Now clutching the papers tightly in her right hand, she hoped her ears had played a trick on her. Her heart sank. They hadn't.

Once again Tate's deep, rich voice assaulted her senses.

"I'm not asking, Ms. Purcell. I'm telling you that I have to see Ms. Lee. Now suppose you tell me where she is."

An assistant was minding Marnie's desk, and Marnie could imagine how intimidated she must be with Tate looming over her, his blue eyes as cold as the Arctic.

So desperate was she to calm her own hammering pulse that she missed the assistant's reply. It didn't matter, however, as the door to Lance's office suddenly flew open.

Marnie stood motionless in some fragile balance between anticipation and fear as Tate O'Brien cleared the threshold and crossed into the room, Stetson in hand.

Startled beyond words, she stared at an altogether different man from the formally dressed stranger of the party. Gone were the slacks and sports coat. In their place were a chambray shirt and Levi's pressed to a sharp crease.

Against his smooth-shaven face, his mustache seemed more prominent than when she'd first met him, and his dark salt-and-pepper hair longer and more mussed. But neither of those imperfections dampened the blatant sexual charisma he exuded. In fact, she wondered what it would be like to kiss a man with a mustache. She wondered what it would be like to kiss Tate O'Brien... *You're losing it, Marnie!*

His eyes were on her; everywhere they touched, her skin felt hot. Refusing to let him see the effect he was having on her, Marnie stepped from behind the massive desk, which was strewn with papers, and walked straight to him.

"Good morning, Mr. O'Brien," she said, trying to keep her voice steady. Dismayed, she realized she sounded out of breath.

Although he lifted an eyebrow slightly at her smooth approach, his harsh features did not relent.

"What can I do for you?" she asked when it became apparent he wasn't going to answer her greeting.

"What do you say we cut the pleasantries and get to the heart of the matter?"

"Oh, and what would that be?" she asked, hugging her icy hands to her sides.

If possible, Tate's features hardened even more. Yet his eyes continued to roam over her, searing her skin. "Oh," he said, mimicking her, "I think you know."

Marnie felt herself panic, but not because of his threatening presence. Her apprehension stemmed solely from the way he was scrutinizing her; it was the same way he'd scrutinized her at the party—with something on his mind other than his son's welfare.

"Look, Mr. O'Brien," Marnie said, gathering her shredded nerves together and trying to ignore the way her nipples had tightened, "I won't be dictated to. I—"

"Somehow I don't think you're in a position to threaten me, Ms. Lee."

Marnie opened her mouth to speak, only to swallow an angry retort. Then spinning around, she made her way to the window on the other side of the room and looked outside, her thoughts racing. She wouldn't let him do this to her. True, she loved her job; she *needed* her job. But there were other jobs in the marketplace, and with her experience she could get another one. *But not one that could offer the same challenge and the money,* she cried silently.

She didn't have to turn around to know that he was behind her. She felt his warm breath on the back of her neck. She shivered as a chill darted through her.

"I want you to leave my son alone."

"Please," she said faintly, "you're blowing this all out of proportion."

"I won't have you marrying him for his money."

She swung around; spots of red in each cheek had replaced the pallor. "How dare you say that? You don't know a thing about me!"

"The hell I don't! I know everything there is to know about you. Remember, you're working on a high-security project, and don't forget I own this place."

"You mean you—you . . . deliberately pulled my file. . . ." The thought of him prying into her life nauseated her.

"That's right, Ms. Lee," he said in the same accusing tone.

"All this because your son took me out a few times?" She had a sudden and overwhelming desire to laugh, to be hysterical about the whole thing. It was so ludicrous.

"We both know it's more than that." His voice cracked like a whip.

Trying hard not to choke, Marnie moved suddenly and quickly away from the window. And him.

Her ploy didn't work. Either he was too furious to pick up on the rebuff or he didn't care. He simply shifted with her.

"How much, Ms. Lee?"

"How much what?"

"Don't play games with me," he said, lowering his voice. It literally vibrated with fury as he went on. "How much money will it take to make you leave my son alone?"

"How dare you!" Marnie cried, raising her hand with every intention of slapping his face.

Tate was too quick; he caught her wrist in midair. They glared at each other in silent rage.

The clock on the wall chimed the hour. Sunlight flooded the room, danced across the furniture. Nearby, someone pounded on a typewriter. In the distance a door slammed shut.

Neither was aware of the sights and sounds around them—only each other. Their chests heaved. Their breaths mingled. Their eyes sparred.

"Oh, why the hell not," Tate muttered, then reached out, jerked her roughly against him and ground his lips onto hers.

Instantly Marnie's heart pounded against her rib cage. Simultaneous sensations of hot and cold gripped her. It was only when she felt his tongue invade her mouth that she came to her senses and began to struggle.

"No!" she whimpered, pushing against his chest.

Gulping for breath, Tate let her go.

For another sizzling moment they stared at each other, their breathing ragged, both unable to cope with what had happened.

"Damn," Tate said, rubbing the back of his neck.

Marnie wrapped her arms around her body and bit down on her lip to steady it.

Finally, after what seemed an eternity, Tate spun around and stamped toward the door. He had his hand on the knob before a word was spoken.

"Don't think for one second this changes anything," he said, his voice harsh with bitterness, "because it doesn't."

The moment the door closed behind him, Marnie managed to stumble to the desk and sink into the chair, fearing she might at any moment lose the contents of her stomach.

Thirty minutes later she was still sitting there.

Four

The wind rattled the windows of the barn like an unwanted visitor.

Tate, however, paid the outside elements scant attention. He was too busy venting his frustrations on the bale of hay in front of him. His heart pounded; sweat popped out on his forehead and upper lip.

His shoulders burned like pokers. Still he jabbed the hay with the pitchfork and heaved it up and forward, sending it sailing from the loft to the floor below. He had stable hands to do this back-breaking chore, but he'd opted to do it himself, thinking it was just the tonic he needed to settle down.

His face, etched in a deep frown as he stripped a

glove from one hand and mopped his brow, continued to mirror his frustration.

It was past time he did some soul-searching, something he hadn't been able to do since he'd grabbed Marnie Lee in a fit of anger and kissed her. Instead he'd concentrated on keeping the dull ache inside him from turning into despair. So far he'd failed miserably.

Over and over in his mind that kiss repeated itself. He remembered every detail of that moment. He remembered the feel of her lips against his, their trembling softness. He remembered the feel of her hard nipples as they were pressed against his chest.

Nothing short of a miracle, he guessed, could wipe that memory from his mind. And now, as before, his body responded, which only added to his confusion; it was something he couldn't recall ever happening.

So what would it be like to make love to her?

No! Never. Not her. Everything that was decent inside him rebelled. He wouldn't compete with his son!

His face grim, Tate shoved the glove back on and stuck another bale of hay, tossing it below. Although he'd asked himself umpteen times why he'd kissed her to start with, he hadn't yet come up with an answer. Nor could he figure out why she triggered both his anger and his libido at the same time.

Hell, he wasn't interested in getting involved with a woman. Affairs only complicated things. For the first time in his life, he was in a position to do exactly as he pleased. His dream of raising and training quarter horses was finally becoming reality.

Yet Marnie Lee had touched something inside him, something heretofore untapped. She made him ache, which was all the more reason to fire her, he told himself, if she failed to heed his warning.

"Hey, watch where you're throwing that stuff, will ya?"

Tate peered over the edge of the loft into the upturned face of his foreman, J. D. Rowe, a big, burly man with a beer belly.

"Sorry," Tate muttered, "didn't hear you come in."

J.D.'s grin was guileless. "Naw, I guess you didn't at that. You were too busy giving that hay bloody hell."

"Is there something you want?" Tate asked pointedly, glaring at him.

J.D.'s grin didn't so much as waver. He merely removed his hat and scratched his head as if he had all the time in the world.

Tate wasn't surprised by his foreman's lack of intimidation. Not only was J.D. the best foreman in these parts, but he was a good friend, as well.

In spite of himself, Tate smiled back and merely waited for his slow-talking foreman to say what he had come to say. He didn't have to wait long.

"Just thought I'd check to see if you wanted me to ride with you over to the Kelly place to look at that mare. If not, I'm going to mend those broken fences in the south pasture."

Tate slammed a palm against the handle of the pitchfork. "Dammit, I forgot about that appointment."

"Well, do you want me to tag along or not?"

"No, you go ahead and take care of the fences. They're more important."

"All right, see you later," J.D. said, turning and shuffling off.

A short time later Tate walked out of the barn, only to stop abruptly and curse.

Fran Hunt, the woman he'd been seeing a lot of lately was strutting toward him. Her face, framed by thick blond hair that fell to her shoulders, was unremarkable, but her body more than compensated for that flaw. Long legs, tiny waist and exquisitely-shaped breasts rounded out the package.

However, she was the last person Tate wanted to see right now.

"Hi, honey," Fran said in a sugary tone, stopping only a hairbreadth away from him.

"Hello, Fran," he answered on a sigh.

Her lower lip protruded. "Is that the best you can do? How about a little kiss."

Unconsciously, Tate stepped back, the thought of kissing her suddenly abhorrent. "Not now, Fran. I'm too dirty." He forced a smile, hoping to take a little of the edge off his rejection.

"Why, honey," she cajoled, sliding her hands up and down the front of his damp shirt, "you never let that stop you before."

With supreme effort, Tate hung on to his temper, trapping her hands, then removing them. "Not now, I said."

Her features hardened. "I don't know why I put up with you. When you want to, you can be a real bastard."

"No one's twisting your arm to stick around."

As if fearing she might have pushed him too far, Fran softened her tone and smiled. "Will I see you tonight?"

"Maybe."

"Well, when you make up your mind, let me know, you hear."

With that she turned and walked to her car. Tate watched while she cranked it and jerked it into gear.

Then blistering the air with another expletive, he stamped toward the house.

"Daddy, I'll see you tomorrow, okay?"

Silas Lee sat statue still in the leather wing chair and continued to stare out the window.

Marnie knew he wasn't seeing the beautiful landscaped grounds that surrounded this special-care facility, just as he hadn't seen her when she'd walked into his room a little while ago. Yet she went through the motions, pretending the disease hadn't robbed him of his mind as well as his dignity, pretending that he understood everything she told him.

Vigorously Marnie blinked back the tears that blurred her vision and gave his frail shoulders another quick hug.

"When I come back tomorrow, I'll bring you some more of your favorite candy." She almost choked on the lump in her throat. "I—I see . . . you're just about out."

Again, no response. He merely looked at her through vacant eyes. After looking at him another long moment, Marnie lifted dejected shoulders and crossed to the door. Once there, she paused and turned around, scanning the room with tear-filled eyes, as if to reassure herself that her beloved had the best that money could buy.

The large, airy room bore all the comforts of home; she had seen to that. Pictures that were special to him adorned the walls and littered the top of the chest of drawers. A braided rug, resting on top of the carpet, added another cheery dimension. Plants on one windowsill added still another.

If she'd had her way, though, he'd be at home with her. Such a move was out of the question; she could no longer handle him. Brushing the painful thought aside, she twisted the knob and whispered, "Good-bye, Daddy."

By the time she made it to the office, Marnie was once again in control of herself. But then, she'd had no choice. She had to bury her problems behind the church-house door, the way her father used to tell her. *Cry, sure, but get past it. Life goes on.*

She had just reached her desk and was staring with remorse at the mound of paperwork on it when Lance entered the room.

"Hi," he said, and perched on one corner of her desk, a wide grin on his handsome face.

"Good morning," Marnie responded.

His grin collapsed. "Is that all you have to say?"

"What did you want me to say?"

"Something other than a grumpy good morning, that's for sure."

Marnie slipped her arms out of the jacket of her peach linen suit and draped it over the back of her chair. "Sorry, but grumpy's the way I feel. I've just come from seeing Silas."

"Any change?" Lance asked, shifting his gaze as if he was uncomfortable.

"No, but thanks for asking anyway."

Lance smiled lamely, then changed the subject. "I have some good news."

Marnie's face brightened. "Oh?"

"Albert and the two other engineers have finally narrowed the design plans for the explosive down to two."

"Oh, Lance, that's wonderful."

"Yeah, but it's about time."

For weeks a core of engineers had been working on various designs that would not only perfect the plastic explosive but perfect it to such a degree that the government would be satisfied. That in itself had proved to be a major sticking point as each design had its pluses as well as minuses.

During this critical period Marnie had been responsible for gathering together the massive amount of paperwork and getting it on to the computer. The information included details describing how each design functioned, how each was maintained and the conditions under which each was to be used.

"Well, don't keep me in suspense," she said at last, when Lance was not forthcoming with any more details.

"They decided to go with the timing device. From now on, it'll be referred to as 'one-off chip.'" He paused and tossed a folder down in front of her. "It's all there. Read it for yourself."

"Do you think Uncle Sam will be pleased?"

Lance stood. "We'll just have to wait and see, won't we?" He grinned his little-boy grin. "But I'm pleased. And I hope to hell Dad will be, too." His face lost its animation. "But then, one never knows about him."

Marnie could testify to that but, of course, she didn't. She never told Lance about the incident in his office, nor did she intend to.

She wished she could wipe it from her own mind. But no matter what she did, she could still feel the imprint of those hard, taut lips grinding against hers. She had seen him only a few times, but already she felt something, some emotion she couldn't identify. And the fact that he was Lance's father and so much older than she didn't come into it.

Suddenly Marnie swallowed against the lump in the back of her throat and turned her head away so that Lance wouldn't see the confusion mirrored in her eyes.

"Marnie?"

She spun her head around. "Sorry," she said, flashing him a bright, apologetic smile for woolgathering.

"I'll pick you up at eight."

Marnie's smile slipped. "Do you think that's a good idea?"

"Sure, why not?"

For some reason his cocky, flippant attitude irritated her. "You know why not," she snapped.

He chuckled, then leaned over and kissed her on the cheek. "If I promise not to mention the word *marriage*, will you let me take you to dinner?"

"Lance—"

"We'll call it a celebration dinner." He angled his head. "Come on, what d'you say?"

Suddenly she thought of Tate's warning. "All right," she said recklessly. "I'll go."

Even for a Friday night the restaurant Lance chose was crowded. The Back Porch was another favorite of Marnie's. She had been here several times with Kate. In addition to the relaxed atmosphere, it had the best salad bar in Houston, along with the best pizza.

Tonight the band in another room was playing a Kenny Rogers oldie. While the waiter filled their wineglasses, Marnie tapped her foot to the music.

They had already ordered. Marnie chose pizza on whole-wheat bread with lots of tangy tomato sauce and good, gooey mozzarella cheese, while Lance decided on the lasagna.

Once the waiter had gone, Lance asked, "Glad you came?"

Marnie smiled. "You know I am."

"Then let's toast to the success of the project, shall we?"

Marnie reached for her glass, only to suddenly stop. The color drained slowly from her face.

Standing in the doorway and staring straight at her was Tate O'Brien.

"Marnie, what's wrong?" Lance demanded. "Are you sick or something? You look like you've seen a ghost."

For another long moment Marnie remained as though caught in a freeze-frame, unable to take her eyes off Tate. It was only after he turned his attention to the woman at his side, the one who'd been with him at the ranch, that Marnie dragged her gaze away from his commanding figure.

Even so, when she faced Lance again, it was Tate's image she saw. Maybe it was the lighting, but Tate's face had appeared a deeper tan than usual, as had his bare arms. His hair, while a trifle unruly, complemented the blue shirt that was unbuttoned far enough to allow a smidgen of chest hair to show. Thighs, muscular and trim, filled his jeans.

"You're not going to faint on me, are you?" Lance was asking.

Marnie smiled bravely, though her stomach was heaving. "It's . . . your father."

"Here?"

"Yes, here." Marnie's voice quivered slightly.

Lance's snort of disgust could not be ignored. Then beginning to mutter under his breath, he swung around.

Tate and his companion were threading their way through the tables toward what Marnie prayed was the veranda. But in order to reach that section of the restaurant, they had to pass beside her table. Her pulse rate climbed.

"I can't imagine what he's doing here," Lance said, his features grim.

Marnie pushed her lips together. "It's simple. He's spying."

Lance opened his mouth to reply, only to suddenly close it as a shadow appeared over the table.

Marnie's mouth went dry. Lance stared at his drink. Neither said a word.

Then Lance raised his head and said, "Hello, Dad."

A thick artery pulsed in Tate's throat. "Son. Ms. Lee."

"What brings you and Fran here?" Lance's tone bordered on hostility. "I never knew you liked pizza."

"There's a lot you don't know about me."

Lance clamped his lips together.

Marnie had purposefully kept her eyes off Tate, opting instead to concentrate on the woman Lance had called Fran. Obviously bored with what was going on at the table, Fran had turned her attention to another one nearby and was chatting with its occupants.

Not bad, Marnie mused to herself cattily, taking in Fran's voluptuous figure.

"Well, you two have a nice evening," Tate was saying, his tone smooth and unaffected.

Marnie jerked her head up, knowing Tate meant for her and Lance to have anything but a nice evening.

"Yeah," Lance said, sarcastically voicing her thought.

In that beat of hesitation that followed, Marnie's eyes locked with Tate's. Something passed between them that had nothing to do with Lance. Color stole slowly up Marnie's face as his gaze suddenly seemed centered on the taut imprint of her breasts, their fullness barely concealed behind the coral knit sweater.

Then, moving his gaze, Tate smiled a cold little smile that wasn't a smile at all. "Ms. Lee."

The instant Tate and Fran walked off, the waitress arrived with Lance and Marnie's food. Once their glasses were refilled, they tried to pretend nothing was wrong. They laughed over small incidents that had taken place at the plant and argued amiably about nothing that mattered.

Marnie made an effort to savor every bite she took, but she could not. The pizza tasted like cardboard. Finally, she gave up and eased the plate aside.

Lance, however, didn't seem to have the same problem. He devoured his lasagna with relish.

"You're not hungry?" Lance asked, pushing his empty plate away.

Marnie casually flicked a hair away from her face. "Guess not."

"Do you mind if I finish it?"

She smiled and shook her head. "Help yourself."

"Well, the way I see it, it's a shame to waste good food."

Marnie, trying her best to forget that Tate was sitting across the room from her and that she was under his baleful eye, focused her attention on Lance. Still, she couldn't rid herself of Tate's annoying presence.

She was aware of him with every heightened nerve in her body.

"Mmm, now that's pizza," Lance said at last, rubbing his stomach. "You don't know what you missed."

"Oh yes, I do." Marnie's voice was low. "I just wasn't as hungry as I first thought."

Lance leaned forward. "Look, don't let my dad get to you. Like I said, his bark is much worse than his bite."

Marnie didn't believe that for a second. Nevertheless, she didn't say anything.

The silence lengthened while they sipped their wine.

Then lowering his glass, Lance blurted, "Marry me, Marnie. Tomorrow."

Marnie stared at him in stunned disbelief.

"We could make it work," Lance went on. "I love you enough for both of us."

"Oh, Lance, you promised you wouldn't bring that up."

Lance shrugged. "Okay, so I broke my promise, but dammit, I want you so much."

"That's because you haven't had me," she countered with blunt honesty.

He flushed. "It's not from lack of trying, that's for damned sure."

Determined to make her case once and for all that marriage between them was impossible, Marnie said, "Your father came to the office the other day."

Instantly Lance tensed. "Where was I?"

"At the attorney's."

"Why didn't you tell me?"

"Because he didn't come to see you. He came to see me."

His jaw dropped open. "You. But why?"

"He told me to leave you alone."

"You're not serious."

"Of course, I'm serious," Marnie snapped.

He flushed again. "Sorry."

"In fact, he tried to buy me off."

"Why...that—"

Marnie leaned forward again and clasped his hand, interrupting him. "It was never my intention to cause trouble. Obviously that's exactly what he thinks I'm doing." She paused and withdrew her hand. "Still, I'm curious if it's just me he doesn't like or if it's any woman who gets close to you."

"Well, I have gotten myself in a couple of jams," Lance admitted grudgingly, "but I've never asked anyone to marry me."

A smile eased the tension around Marnie's lips. "And don't think I'm not honored that you asked me, because I am. But I don't love you, Lance, and I don't think you love me. And I don't think we should see each other outside the office any more." She paused again and drew in a shuddering breath. "I can't afford to lose my job."

"Did my father threaten you? Is that what this is all about?"

Marnie shifted uneasily, unable to meet his direct gaze. "Let's just say we didn't part on the best of terms and leave it at that."

"Well, I hope you told him where to get off, because if you didn't I intend to."

"No, Lance," Marnie said emphatically. "Enough is enough. He thinks what he's doing is right, and who am I to argue? After all, look what a good job you're doing on this project." Dropping her gaze, she stared at him from under her lashes. "Let it go, Lance. Just let it go."

Lance didn't look at all convinced. "All right, Marnie. You win for now. But I'm not giving up. You can mark that down, and this, as well—I can handle my father because he needs me, needs me to do the job he no longer wants to do. So you see, you don't have a thing to worry about."

No, you're wrong, she cried silently. *Dead wrong. No one handles Tate O'Brien.*

Later, when she and Lance got up to leave the restaurant, Marnie vowed she wouldn't look at Tate. She looked anyway. But he was too busy laughing at something Fran was saying to notice her scrutiny.

With cheeks ablaze, Marnie followed Lance outside onto the deserted street corner, then toward his car that was parked on a side street. Preoccupied, they walked in silence.

The night was gorgeous, Marnie thought. The sky was thickly populated with stars. After a moment of stargazing, Marnie paused, took a deep breath and wished she could stop thinking about Tate.

So caught up was she in nursing her inner turmoil that she failed to notice the car easing to the curb until it was too late.

The vehicle's door flew open, and a masked man jumped out with the quickness of lightning. Before either she or Lance could turn around, the man lunged for Lance and began dragging him toward the car.

Marnie, paralyzed with fear and shock, couldn't move, couldn't speak. Then recovering with an alacrity born of desperation, she screamed a blood-curdling scream. "Lance! Oh, my God, Lance!"

Lance fought. "Run, Marnie, run!" he cried weakly before his assailant slapped a cloth against his face.

"Let him go!" Marnie cried, tearing after them.

"Shut up, lady," the man ground out as he pushed Lance, who was now deadweight, into the front seat.

"Stop it!" Marnie shouted.

The man paid her no heed.

Physically she knew she was no match for the man's brute strength, but that didn't stop her. Suddenly and unexpectedly, she attacked him from behind, dragging her nails across his bare, tender scalp.

He swore loudly, but then recovered his equilibrium and tried to still her hands.

"Dammit, lady!"

Though her breath was lodged in her throat and hot tears almost blinded her, she refused to let go of the man. She balled her fingers into a fist and slammed them against the man's head. Once. Twice. Three times.

"You bastard, let—"

She got no further. The man whipped around and whacked the side of her head. For a split second the blow stifled Marnie's effort. But then she shook her head and charged him again, grabbing his mask. On contact, it partially split. For a heart-stopping moment, Marnie was eye-to-eye with the man.

Then sobbing, she staggered backward.

"Stop her, you idiot," the man behind the wheel shouted. "Get her, too."

With both hands now free, Lance's assailant reached for Marnie grabbing her arms with fingers that felt like steel traps.

Her breath hurt in her lungs. Her face throbbed where she'd been hit. Her arms ached from hitting him. Still, she fought like a wild, wounded animal.

She wouldn't let them take Lance. She wouldn't let them take *her*. But time was against her. She begged her body not to let her down.

The man's savage strength gave him the upper hand. Marnie felt hers slowly drain from her body. She knew it would be only a matter of seconds before she would be forced inside the car along with Lance.

Voices. Had she heard voices? Yes. And feet, feet pounding the cement. Her heart leaped.

"Help me," she sobbed, trying desperately to break his hold on her.

"Let her go!" the man's cohort yelled. "We gotta get outta here!"

Those words barely registered on Marnie's numbed mind, but what did register was the hard shove she received from behind.

"Oh, God," she whimpered, grappling to maintain her balance.

"Marnie! Marnie!"

She looked up in silent agony. *Tate!* she mouthed, just as she made contact with the pavement and felt its roughness rip the skin from her knees.

Five

"Oh, Tate," Marnie sobbed, clinging to him as he lifted her, torn and bleeding, to her feet. "Lance . . . you've got to help. He—" She broke off, her breath coming in short, gutsy spurts.

"Marnie, where's Lance?" Tate's voice, close to her ear, had a scraping, tearing edge to it. "Was he in the car that drove off?"

Marnie stood and stared at him as if in a stupor, waiting for her mind to function. Nothing came, nothing but horror. She was shaking. She had to make herself believe this was real. She had to control the shock reeling through her.

Tate's grip on her shoulder tightened. "Lance," he

shouted. Then, his features contorting, he shouted again, "Where's Lance?"

It was the panic in his voice that eventually penetrated Marnie's numbed senses. She finally managed to groan, "They—they took Lance."

"Bastards!"

Marnie shook her head miserably. "I—I tried to help him, only I couldn't." Her voice once again faded into a pale, childlike wail. "They—they tried to take me, too."

"Who are they?" His tone was frantic now, and he was all but shaking her.

"Two men. They—they took him and drove off."

She heard his horrified gasp. Then he ran his hands up and down her arms. "Are you all right?"

"I'm...fine," she lied, trying not to think about the searing pain in her legs.

He pushed her to arm's length. "No, you're not," he said, looking down. Blood had saturated her panty hose at the knees and was dripping down her legs.

With a muttered curse, Tate led her toward the door of the restaurant. Ashen and shaking, Marnie clung to his hand while mass confusion reigned.

The Back Porch had emptied. Its patrons were outside, wide-eyed and whispering. Passersby had stopped, as well, and were gawking. A siren screamed in the breezy night air.

Once inside the restaurant, Tate eased Marnie down onto a padded bench. Grim faced, he looked up into the hovering manager's face.

"Did someone call the police?"

"Yes, sir," the man answered. "We called the paramedics, too."

"Thanks," Tate muttered, then turned his attention back to Marnie, who was once again staring at him through glazed eyes.

Without removing his gaze from her, Tate dug into his back pocket and pulled out a handkerchief. Then he knelt and dabbed very gently at the blood oozing from a wound.

"Oh, please, don't," Marnie whispered, feeling as if she might faint at any moment, the pain was so severe.

Tate immediately stopped. "Sorry."

"Mr. O'Brien, the police are here," the manager said from his position by the door.

"About damn time."

Tate had no more than gotten the words out of his mouth when two uniformed men walked through the door and introduced themselves as Officers Taylor and Barnhardt.

"My son has been kidnapped," Tate said without mincing words. "Ms. Lee was a witness to it."

Taylor, the older and the shorter of the two, turned to Marnie. "Please tell us what happened."

In a halting voice, Marnie told them exactly what she'd told Tate, and more. Through it all, Tate stood quietly by her side, his face looking as if it were carved out of stone. But his eyes were anything but stonelike. They were narrowed slits filled with outrage.

When she finished speaking, she peered up at him. "I—I'm so sorry. If only I'd . . ."

A thick, knotty artery stood out in his neck. "Don't blame yourself."

But for some crazy reason Marnie did blame herself. She knew how desperate, how helpless Tate must be feeling, and her heart went out to him.

Officer Barnhardt cleared his throat, then spoke soothingly. "Mr. O'Brien is there anything you can add to what Ms. Lee has told us?"

"Not much, I'm afraid." Frustrated, Tate ran a hand over his forehead.

"Where were you when the kidnapping took place?"

"I was in the restaurant, at the back of the veranda. By the time I heard the commotion and got down to the street, it was after the fact. I saw only the man's back as he jumped into the getaway car."

Tate paused and focused his attention on Marnie. "Look, can we dispense with the questioning for now and get Ms. Lee some medical attention?"

"Of course," Barnhardt said hurriedly. "We'll radio ahead and have someone meet you at Ben Taub."

The next hour passed in a blur for Marnie. She didn't know how she got to the emergency room, nor did she care. She just knew that Tate never left her side, and for that she was grateful.

It was only after a kind-faced doctor entered the small, sterile cubbyhole that reeked of antiseptic and applied medicine to her wounds, that she rallied.

"Sorry, Ms. Lee," Dr. Evans said when Marnie bit down on her lower lip to keep from crying out. "But these are nasty abrasions and have to be tended to."

Marnie perched on the edge of the cotlike bed and closed her eyes just as the room began to spin.

"Has she fainted, doctor?" Tate asked, his tone anxious.

"I'm . . . sick to my stomach, that's all," Marnie whispered.

Before Tate could respond, the door swung open and two sober-faced men walked in. The one who flashed the badge and introduced himself as FBI agent Stan Courtney was tall and thin with an abundance of rust-red hair flaring around his clean-shaven face. His partner, Agent Mike James, was short and round, with blond hair that was not long enough to be stylish, but long enough to look as though he needed a haircut.

They could have passed for Mutt and Jeff, Marnie thought, battling an overwhelming desire to laugh, to dissolve into hysteria.

Stan Courtney was the first to speak. "I know how difficult this is for you," he said, focusing his gaze on Marnie, "but I have to ask you to repeat what happened."

"All right." The words were barely audible. Once again tears flooded her dark eyes.

"Make it short, Officer," Dr. Evans put in. "She's been through enough for one night."

His lips set in a thin, taut line, Tate stepped closer, as if to protect her, but he didn't say anything. Marnie flashed him a grateful look, then retold her story.

James folded his arms across his chest. "So you got a look at one of the men."

Marnie nodded.

"Think you could ID him?"

"It—it was dark. I'm not sure." At the moment she wasn't sure about much of anything, except that this was turning into a nightmare without an end. She felt the tears well up and winked in rapid succession to keep them back.

Courtney wrote furiously, then turned to Tate. "Mr. O'Brien, we need to know everything there is to know about your son. Do you have any idea who would want to harm him and why? Is there anyone in his business or his household whom you might have reason to suspect?"

"The household is out. My son lives alone." Tate's voice was tight and controlled. "But the possibility of his kidnapping being job-related is very real."

"Oh?" Mike James chimed in. "What makes you say that?"

Tate explained in detail the project Marnie and Lance were working on.

James swung his eyes to Marnie. "Can you add anything to this?"

Marnie swayed.

"Enough, gentlemen," Tate said in a curt tone, stepping forward, his eyes fixed on Marnie's drained, waxen face.

Both agents looked as if they wanted to argue, but then they acquiesced.

"All right, Mr. O'Brien," Courtney said on a sigh, "take Ms. Lee home. But both of you be downtown in the morning. We'll cover everything from our end—

wiretaps, et cetera. Within the next twenty-four hours you'll more than likely hear from the kidnappers."

"No problem. We'll be there."

During the next few minutes silence wrapped itself around the room while Marnie accepted two pain pills and a cup of water from the doctor. Then, with the help of Tate and Dr. Evans, she stood and began a slow trek toward the door.

"Easy does it," Tate murmured, placing his hand on the door knob.

"Ms. Lee."

All three stopped and turned around.

"Do you have somewhere you can stay the rest of the night?" Barnhardt asked.

"Are you saying that she shouldn't stay alone?" Tate demanded bluntly.

"That's exactly what I'm saying. They know or at least think she can identify them, so..." He let his voice play out, but the meaning was clear.

If possible, Marnie turned paler. "I...have a friend who can stay with me."

"Good." Courtney almost smiled. "And for precaution, we'll have an officer posted at your home."

Tate waved an impatient hand. "That won't be necessary."

"Why is that?"

"Ms. Lee will be staying at my ranch."

Marnie stared up at him and gasped.

"No."

"This is not up for discussion, Marnie."

"For the second and last time, I will not pack a bag and go to your ranch."

They were in the living room of her condo. Marnie rested against the bar while Tate stood in the middle of the room, his posture rigid. She didn't want, didn't *need* this confrontation. Weariness, mixed with the pain from her fall, had left her with a dull throb behind her eyes. All she wanted was to crawl into bed.

During the fifteen-minute drive to her house from the hospital, they had scarcely spoken a word to each other. Even so, she'd been aware that Tate's thoughts were as tormented as her own. Would they ever see Lance alive again?

His blue eyes seemed to drill into her. "Dammit, I'm in no mood to argue with you."

"Nor I with you," Marnie said, tears perilously close.

Her weakness and inability to function were not lost on Tate. He made an aggravated groan and stepped forward, only to suddenly stop, as if finding some last minute control.

"Either you call your friend and she comes over or you go with me." Without waiting for a reply, he strode to the phone, lifted the receiver and held it out. "What's it going to be?" Something hard had crept into his eyes, something Marnie dared not ignore.

Trembling violently, she took the receiver and punched out Kate's number. When she heard the answering machine click on, her heart sank. Kate was on a flight.

"She's not home," Marnie whispered, suddenly feeling so exhausted she thought she might die.

"Come on, I'll help you pack."

Her face crumpled. "Please...don't..." She turned away, again struggling to keep the tears at bay. She knew she was behaving terribly and hated herself for it.

As if he sensed she was close to the edge, Tate stood where he was for a moment, his expression brooding and uncertain. "All right, Marnie, you win. I'll stay here."

She stared at him as tremor after tremor rocked her body. He looked composed, so together, so unrelenting, as if he was afraid to show that he was as frightened about Lance as she was.

He should be the one crying, not her. She knew he was hurting. Suddenly she longed to throw her arms around him and tell him that everything was going to be all right, but she couldn't because she was afraid nothing was ever going to be all right again.

His gaze left hers and he scanned the room. "The couch'll do just fine."

"I have a guest bedroom." Marnie spoke barely above a whisper.

Their eyes met again and held.

"I'll be fine here," he said tightly.

Forcing her gaze off him, Marnie made her way to the door, where she paused and turned around. "Do...you think they will..." Her voice broke on a sob.

A flicker of pain crossed his face. "I don't know. We'll just have to wait and see, won't we?"

Unlike Marnie, Tate made no effort to sleep. There was too much to do. Despite the hour, he called his assistant the minute Marnie left and told him what had happened. He then asked him not only to see about Lance's car that was still parked outside the restaurant, but to call and make sure Fran had gotten home. At some point amidst the confusion, he had told Fran to get a cab.

Once he hung up from talking to Neal, he sat on the couch and placed his head in his hands. Later he had no idea how long he had stayed in that position, but he didn't care. It was only after he felt the wetness in his palms that he got up and walked to the window.

Staring out into the inky blackness, he gave in to the multitude of emotions ripping through him. He cursed. He ranted. He raved. He agonized. But most of all, he prayed.

Nothing seemed to help. A terrible sense of loss possessed him.

Lance. His son. He still couldn't believe Lance had been kidnapped, even though he'd lived with this fear since he had made his first million.

Tate closed his eyes and drew on a long breath. Suddenly a memory of he and Lance fishing on the side of a creek bank came to mind. Lance had been four years old.

"Looky, Dad, what I catched," he'd said, holding up a fish that hadn't been much bigger than his hand.

"That's great, son," Tate remembered saying with a wide grin, ruffling Lance's hair. "You're doing great."

Tate's heart twisted in pain as guilt settled over him.

And to think he still had to tell his mother. That thought didn't bear thinking about either. She adored her grandson as much as she adored Tate.

Damn those bastards to hell! He could feel hate pour out of his body like dirty sweat. When, not if, those slimeballs were apprehended, he'd make sure they paid. No liberal judge was going to let them off on a technicality or give them a slap on the wrist.

Meanwhile, if they so much as tried to hurt Marnie again, he'd . . . *Whoa, O'Brien. . . .*

But when he'd lifted her, torn and bleeding off the pavement, he'd felt fear. He'd felt anger. But most of all, he'd felt a tightness in the back of his throat.

The feeling was crazy, he knew, and one he didn't understand or want.

Especially now.

Marnie rolled over on her side. "Ouch!" she yelped under her breath, feeling as though every bone, every muscle in her body had been pummelled with a baseball bat.

It could be worse, she reminded herself. She could have been held captive in some airless closet. Or she could be dead. That sobering thought brought her eyes open, along with all the horrifying events of the previous evening. Tate. Was he still occupying her couch?

After she'd left him standing in the middle of her living room, she'd gone to her room, discarded her bloody shirt along with her other clothing, stepped in the shower, then crawled into bed, all with zombielike coordination. It was as if she'd put her brain on autopilot and merely done what had been required of her.

When she'd closed her eyes, however, she hadn't experienced that blessed relief of deep sleep. Instead, her mind had jumped into gear.

But it hadn't been Lance's stricken face that had filled her mind. It had been Tate's. And with it had come questions she couldn't answer. Why had he refused to leave her? Why hadn't he said to hell with her hardheadedness and walked out?

Now, in the clarity of daylight, the answers to those questions still eluded her.

She had always prided herself on her ability to see what made a person tick. But in a matter of days, Tate had succeeded in undermining that ability. And she knew to try to understand him would be next to impossible.

Groaning, she turned toward the clock on the bedside table and saw that it was not quite seven. With all Tate had to take care of, he had probably left an hour ago.

Eying her robe on the end of the bed, she eased herself up and reached for it. Until she had that first cup of coffee, she couldn't bear to think about what lay ahead of her. After a short stint in the bathroom, she padded barefoot into the living area, only to suddenly stop midstride.

Tate hadn't left. He was stretched out on the couch. She crept closer. From where she stood, she couldn't see anything but the back of his head and an arm dangling off the side.

Blinking against the morning sunlight, Marnie inched still closer. It was only after she reached the end of the sofa and had him in full view that she froze. Not only was he sound asleep, but he was naked—at least from the waist up.

Her cheeks on fire, Marnie jerked her eyes up to his face. But she didn't fare much better there. A day's growth of beard stained his tanned cheeks, making them darker, hollow. Lines surrounded his mouth and eyes, lines that she hadn't noticed before. Yet he looked relaxed. And defenseless. How wrong—on both counts.

There was nothing relaxed or defenseless about Tate O'Brien. He'd written the book on energy, grit and perseverance.

Suddenly he breathed deeply, causing his stomach muscles to ripple. Dazed, she continued to stare without conscience.

His chest, wide and covered with salt-and-pepper, wiry hair, tapered perfectly into a flat, hard stomach comprised of nothing but muscle. Her nerves taut, a breathless feeling in her chest, she stared lower, lingering on his navel, made visible by his low-riding jeans.

She wondered what the rest of him looked like and her heart pounded. Her nipples tightened, and she worried briefly that they would protrude through her gown and robe. Her limbs felt suddenly boneless.

He was attractive, dangerously attractive. A woman would be a fool to get mixed up with him. Still, like a flower drawn to the sun, she was drawn to him. Graphic thoughts of what it would be like to have his lips on hers without hurtful pressure made her insides quiver with suppressed longing.

Tate stirred again. Then, unexpectedly, as if he knew he was being watched, his eyes popped open.

Stunned black eyes locked with her shocked blue ones. The moment was electric as each forgot for a brief time the circumstances that brought them together.

Tate's eyes searched and held her. For the longest moment he didn't seem able to turn away. Rich color flooded Marnie's cheeks at the fervor in his gaze. Her lips parted on a panicked breath.

A heartbeat passed, followed by another. Then, as if reality suddenly struck him like a blow, Tate's expression hardened. "Sorry," he muttered roughly, and reached for his shirt.

An ache ripped at her insides. *For looking at me with something other than hate?* she demanded silently. Aloud she said, "Why?"

He threw her another look. "For not being up and dressed."

She strove to make her voice as light as his. "That's all right. Under...the circumstances, you needed the sleep."

"No," he said emphatically, "under the circumstances, I *didn't* need to sleep."

"Tate...I—"

His eyes were on her lips. "Save it, Marnie."

A hot flush climbed her cheeks. "I—"

He cut her off again. "While I'm at my mother's telling her about...Lance, you get dressed. I'll be back shortly to take you downtown."

"I can drive myself."

He cursed roundly. "Don't argue with me—at least not this morning. Look," he spoke now with extreme patience, as if he were talking to a child, "I know you're sore all over, so just make it easy on yourself and let me drive you. I have to be there, anyway. I've thought of something that might help them find Lance."

Her lips parted as she met his level gaze. "All right, I'll be ready."

He looked at her a second longer than necessary, then turned and walked out the door.

After locking it behind him, Marnie leaned against it, feeling the sting of tears. Lance. Her every thought should have been on him instead of on Tate and how he made her feel.

Hopefully God would forgive her, because she couldn't forgive herself.

Marnie had dreaded the second confrontation with the FBI. But since she'd wanted so desperately to be instrumental in helping find Lance, she was doing her best to cooperate. But it wasn't proving to be easy.

As promised, Tate had returned to pick her up. Determined to give her frantic mind and her sagging spirits a lift, she had dressed with care in gold linen pants, off-white shell and matching jacket.

Still, nothing short of a miracle could erase the dark circles under her eyes or reshape the downward pull of her lips. Yesterday had changed her. But then, one didn't fight off a kidnapper and not feel its effects. Her life would never be the same; *she* would never be the same.

Nor would Tate. Although he'd appeared remarkably fresh in slacks and a striped sports shirt, there had been no denying the gaunt, drawn look on his face.

They had been just a few blocks away from the FBI headquarters before Marnie broke the silence. "I guess it would be safe to assume there has been no word from the kidnappers."

He kept his eyes on the road. "No, not yet," he said tightly, "though all the phone lines in the house are being monitored."

"How's your mother?"

He faced her briefly. "Not good. The doctor had to give her a sedative."

"She hadn't heard before you got there, had she?" Marnie's voice quavered slightly; she felt another twinge of guilt because he hadn't gone home last night.

"No, thank God. So now you don't have to feel guilty any longer."

"Who said I'm feeling guilty?" she said hotly.

"Aren't you?"

A wave of color swept her cheeks. "No one forced you to stay with me, you know."

"No, that's right, they didn't." His voice was an explosive growl.

"Then why did you? Stay, I mean?" The words sounded before she could think to keep quiet.

He faced her again. His blue eyes appeared hollow, as if there were nothing inside him. "I wish to hell I knew."

That had stung, but she hadn't said anything, opting to hold onto that silence even after they had entered FBI headquarters and she'd looked around. The offices were typical. Crowded. Bustling with activity. Sterile, uncomfortable furniture. Cabinets and desks littered with files.

Now, as she stood behind the computer screen and listened to the artist's instructions, Marnie inhaled deeply and tried to clear her mind of everything, everything except the kidnapper's face. But it was no use; his features remained hazy and unclear.

"It's all right, Ms. Lee," Stan Courtney said. "Just take your time."

Marnie frowned. "I was positive I could remember what he looked like, and now..." Her voice faded as she turned anxiously toward Tate, who was standing slightly behind her.

Tate's eyebrows were also drawn together in a heavy frown that lightened only marginally when he spoke. "Maybe you're trying too hard. Or maybe the doctor's prediction came true."

"And what is that, Mr. O'Brien?" Mike James asked, stubbing out his cigarette in the ashtray he was holding in his hand.

"She is unable to recall due to the trauma she suffered."

Both James and Courtney turned their scrutiny on Marnie.

"Do you feel like that's what's happening, Ms. Lee?" Courtney asked.

Marnie dragged in a shuddering breath. "I don't know. But I...suppose it could be true." Then turning to Tate, she added, "I'm...sorry."

"Yeah, me too."

Silence fell over the small group.

Courtney coughed. "Well, we'll just have to keep the faith that you'll remember."

In spite of her efforts to appear composed, Marnie's lower lip trembled. "I just pray it won't be too late," she finally said, sick at heart. Not only had she let Lance down, but she had let Tate down, as well.

"It won't," Agent James said with far more confidence than the situation warranted. Nevertheless, Marnie was grateful and gave him a small smile.

After coughing again, James switched his attention to Tate. "If it was the plastic explosive they wanted, why not simply steal the plans?"

"Who knows what these crazy terrorists do or why they do it?" Tate said grimly. "But my guess is that the plans are no good without someone to interpret them."

"And your son can do that?"

"No."

James's eyes narrowed. "Then why the hell did they take him?"

"I'm assuming they didn't know that." Tate's tone was crisp but patient.

James blew his breath out and raked a hand through his hair. "Ah, so you think that if Lance keeps them thinking he can reconstruct the design, his chances of staying alive are good?"

"That's what I'm hoping for, unless..." Tate paused, and this time it was he who plowed his fingers through his hair.

Marnie, watching him, had to again fight the urge to run to him, fling her arms around his neck and comfort him.

"Unless what, Mr. O'Brien?" James pressed, his eyes alert.

"Unless Lance was kidnapped for some other reason."

James's tone of voice did not alter. "And what might that reason be?"

"Lance was almost kidnapped once when he was five years old," Tate said. "It was an extortion attempt, and though the attempt was foiled, I've lived in dread of that happening again."

"I see," Courtney said, entering the conversation and gnawing at the side of his jaw. "Well either way, without Ms. Lee's description, we don't have a lot to go on."

All eyes swung to Marnie.

Her chin jutted. "I'll remember," she said. "I have no choice."

"In the meantime," Courtney said, looking at both Marnie and Tate, "I want to know all there is to know, the latest firings in the company, disgruntled employees, rivalries, forgotten enemies and grudge-bearing friends."

Three hours later they walked out of FBI headquarters.

"I'll come in with you."

Tate had just killed the engine of his Porsche and sat facing Marnie. They were parked in front of her condo.

She shook her head and reached for the door handle. Suddenly the confines of the interior were too close. *Tate* was too close. She could see the smooth plane of his jaw, see the way the hairs curled thickly on the back of his hands, smell his cologne.

"Thanks, but that's not necessary," she said unevenly. "You heard Agent Courtney. He said my place would be crawling with plainclothesmen."

"*Would*. That's just the point."

"All right," Marnie said, too tired to argue.

His eyes widened, and he almost smiled.

"Surprised, huh?"

This time he smiled for real. "That you didn't argue? Very."

The change the smile made was startling. Marnie almost gasped aloud. Instead, she averted her gaze and quickly got out of the car.

Her thoughts were elsewhere as she preceded him inside, so when she looked up it hit her suddenly.

"Oh, no!" she cried, freezing in her tracks.

"What the h—" Tate got no further.

The room was a complete wreck. The wicker furniture was slashed to ribbons, the cushions ripped, their stuffing strewn around the room like snowdrifts. There was black paint splashed everywhere. Her cassette tapes and records had been taken out of their sleeves and either bent, broken or scored with something like a fork.

Her books were off the shelves and looked as if they had been chopped with an ax and left to bleed.

"This settles it," Tate muttered savagely from behind her. "You're coming to the ranch with me."

Six

If Marnie had still harbored any illusions that she might not be in danger, she couldn't doubt her situation any longer as she stood in the guest bedroom at Tate's ranch.

A light springtime rain was falling softly, coating the leaves outside the window with a thick, shiny sheen. The weather matched her mood, she thought, swallowing the lump in her throat, the lump that had been there since earlier today when she had walked into her condo and found it trashed.

Feeling suddenly weak again, Marnie sank into the nearest chair and closed her eyes, hoping to block out the vivid pictures of the devastation that had been her home. Her efforts were in vain. The sight of her furniture slashed, her things strewn, mangled and broken, would haunt her forever.

Tears stung her eyes, forcing her to open them again. She was scared, scared that the men who had taken Lance wouldn't stop until they had her in their clutches, as well. But what frightened her as much, if not more, was that she was now under Tate's roof, under his watchful eye.

What was there about this enigma of a man that had her so out of sorts? She had enough problems without adding a fervent fascination with a man who felt nothing but animosity toward her. Physical attraction—was that at the root of the fascination? More to the point, was it sex? The *lack* of it?

Angry, she got up and walked to the window. She'd admit there were times when she was lonely, yearned for someone to cuddle against at night, to talk over the events of her day, to share her problems with. But those feelings were fleeting and far between.

Besides, she'd been hooked once, shortly before her father was diagnosed, on an older man, an attorney who turned out to be married with two children. She'd been devastated, but because of Silas she'd had to pull herself up by the bootstraps and tend to him.

In the following years she had come to terms with both her past affair and her father's illness and was content with her life. Until now. Until Tate O'Brien had entered it. And to think she'd let him lead her to his house like a docile, unsuspecting lamb to the slaughter. But what choice had she had?

When Tate had blurted that order, she had been so overwrought she hadn't been able to think clearly, much less argue.

After one more incredulous look around the condo, Tate had spoken again, his voice as cold and sharp as a razor. "Come on, let's get the hell outta here."

Once they had turned their backs on the devastation and hate, they had walked outside and stopped. Marnie had sat on the top step of the porch, while Tate stood beside her.

They had remained there for a long time, perfectly still and perfectly quiet. Then Tate, with a muttered curse, had gone next door to use the telephone.

Courtney and James hadn't let them go back inside the condo until the forensic team was through with its investigation. Marnie had waited in the back seat of the agents' unmarked car while a tight-lipped Tate had paced up and down the sidewalk, furious because they had refused to let him inside the building.

"It's mostly the living room," Courtney had said a short time later, lighting a cigarette and taking a deep puff. "Needless to say, Ms. Lee, you won't be able to stay at home."

"She's staying at my place," Tate said, looking at Marnie.

"That's a good idea," Courtney replied, his eyes shifting between the two of them.

"Why would someone want to do something like that?" Marnie asked in a faraway voice.

"That's a damn good question," Tate put in harshly.

Courtney shrugged, then flipped his unsmoked cigarette to the ground and crushed it with his shoe. "I figured they broke in to either take Ms. Lee or to scare the hell out of her. Or both. And when she wasn't home, they vented their frustrations."

Tate's face looked gray. "Or maybe it was a warning of things to come?"

"Could be," Courtney said.

"Oh, God," Marnie whispered, her gaze on Tate. "Is—is this ever going to end?"

For a moment Tate's gaze softened, as if the threadbare look on her face had gotten to him. Then his features hardened and he said, "Possibly when you remember what the piece of slime looked like."

All the remaining color drained from Marnie's face, and she flinched, feeling as if Tate had punched her in the stomach. Then she rallied, boiling fury consuming her. "Don't you think I'm trying?" she lashed out.

A deep silence fell.

Once again Courtney's eyes jockeyed between Tate and Marnie, looking as if he wanted to say something to relieve the tension, but didn't know how.

But in the end it was Courtney who broke the silence. "Look, no one's to blame here," he said, taking another cigarette out of his pocket and lighting it. Then focusing his gaze on Tate exclusively, he added, "Both your office phones and your home phones are tapped. You should be hearing something soon. Based on that, we'll make our move accordingly."

"Don't patronize me, Courtney." Tate's bitterness was tangible. "We both know the chances of my son getting out of this alive are not—"

Staring at him, Marnie started to choke.

Tate returned her stare for an aching moment, then muttered another expletive and looked away.

Before anyone had a chance to speak again, the front door opened. Mike James stood on the step. "All through in here, Stan."

Tate turned to Marnie. "Come on, let's get your things and go."

"And in the meantime," Courtney said, sounding relieved, "if it's all right with you, Ms. Lee, I'll call a firm I know who can come around and clean up the mess—they specialize in vandalized houses. I suppose your insurance will cover everything."

"I . . . hope so," Marnie said, getting out of the car and forcing herself to walk with Tate up the sidewalk.

Once they reentered the house, Marnie moved like a robot through the debris to her room, where she packed a bag as quickly as her unsteady hands would allow.

The trip to the ranch was made in virtual silence as she leaned her head back, pretending to rest. She didn't have anything to say to Tate, anyway, especially after his brutal comment pertaining to her inability to identify the kidnapper.

Annie met them at the door with red-rimmed eyes and a lower lip that wouldn't stop trembling.

"Oh, Tate," she wailed, "what are we going to do?"

"Everything that's possible is being done, Annie," Tate said gently, giving her outstretched hands a squeeze.

"I just can't believe it," she wailed again, resting her eyes briefly on Marnie. "I just can't believe it. My precious Lance—"

"Annie," Tate interrupted, "Ms. Lee's going to be our guest for a while. Her house was broken into and vandalized."

Annie's hand flew to her mouth. "Oh, no. You poor dear. Well, don't you fret. No one will bother you here. I'll see to that."

Tate patted her on the shoulder. "Good girl. I knew I could count on you."

Marnie dug deep for a smile. "Thanks, Annie."

The housekeeper followed them to the guest bedroom and pulled back the shutter while Tate set her bags on the chest at the foot of the bed.

"Would you care for something refreshing to drink?" Annie asked, her hand on the doorknob.

"Not right now, Annie. I just want to freshen up and rest for a while."

"Well, if you need anything don't hesitate to ask."

An awkward silence followed Annie's exit. Marnie refused to meet Tate's eyes.

"Marnie."

Startled by the unexpected use of her name, she looked up but still refused to meet his gaze.

"You'll be all right, won't you?" he asked, his voice sounding raw, as if the words were ripped from his throat.

"Do you really care?" she retorted.

For a moment they simply looked at each other, the air sizzling between them. Marnie felt a jumble of emotions too complex to analyze.

Finally Tate muttered, "I'm going to the office. I'll be back later."

That conversation had taken place over thirty minutes ago, and she still hadn't freshened up or rested. Swallowing a sigh, she stood and walked to the window and looked outside, determined to put aside thoughts of Tate and the tragic circumstances that had forced them together.

Directly in her line of vision was a well-manicured lawn that extended as far as the eye could see, a lawn littered with trees of all sizes and shapes—oaks, sweet gums and Chinese tallows.

Farther to her left was a large barn with a concrete addition and another long building. A sturdy post fence that eventually turned into barbed wire disappeared into the huge pasture dotted with Tate's prized quarter horses.

The tranquil beauty, while not awesome, was certainly heart-stopping. She watched the horses graze for a moment longer, then turned wearily away. If she didn't sit down soon, she knew she'd fall down. She couldn't remember ever being this exhausted.

She eased down onto the side of the bed and released a long, pent-up sigh.

The decor of the room, like the rest of the house, was luxurious but warm. The walls were painted an off white, and the floor was covered with thickly piled peach carpet. A queen-size bed dominated one end of the room and was topped with a peach-flowered comforter. The single chest and night stands were walnut.

Her condo was nice, but it couldn't compare with this luxury, which only emphasized the difference in her and Tate's stations in life.

She sighed again and leaned back on the bed, only to suddenly sit back up.

"Ms. Lee."

"What is it, Annie?"

"I'm sorry to disturb you, but there's someone here to see you. A Ms. McCall."

Kate!

Smiling, Marnie shuffled to the door and gladly opened it. "Where is she?"

"In the den."

"Thanks," Marnie said warmly, and made her way very gingerly down the hall.

When she reached the large room, Kate was perched on the edge of a chair, her blue eyes wide and uncertain.

"Kate McCall, you're the last person I expected to see," Marnie said, meeting her friend halfway and hugging her tightly.

After a moment Kate stepped back and asked, "Why? The minute I turned on my machine and got your message, I had to see for myself that you were all right."

Marnie suddenly felt like crying. "Well, as you can see, I'm still in one piece, though barely. But I couldn't leave my condo without letting both you and the nursing home know where I was."

"Are you sure you didn't dream this nightmare?"

Marnie pointed to her slacks-covered knees. "You want me to show you the damage?"

Kate shuddered. "I get the picture. Anyway, your face says it all. If I cut your throat, I doubt you'd bleed a drop."

"Probably wouldn't."

"Let's sit down," Kate said. "There's so much I don't know."

As best she could, Marnie told her friend everything that had happened after she and Lance had walked out of the restaurant.

When Marnie finished, Kate's face was as pale as Marnie's. "God, what if Lance—"

"Please, don't say it," Marnie cried. "Don't even think it."

"What does his father think?"

Marnie toyed with a strand of hair. "We haven't discussed it. It's...something neither one of us has been able to talk about."

"There's no word from the kidnappers yet, I take it?"

"Zilch," Marnie said flatly.

Kate smacked the palm of her hand. "Of all the blessed times to get called out."

"Don't blame yourself. Tate...spent the night on my couch."

Kate raised her eyebrows. "Tate? You mean Lance's old man stayed with you?"

Marnie flushed. "If you could see him, you wouldn't exactly call him old."

Kate's eyebrows rose even higher.

"Don't say what you're thinking," Marnie snapped. "You couldn't be more wrong. Tate O'Brien wouldn't throw water on me if I were on fire."

"Then why are you here?"

"Believe me, it's not by choice. The FBI said I couldn't stay at my condo."

Kate smiled. "You can stay with me."

"How, when you won't be there?"

"Oh, but I will. I'm starting a three-week vacation tomorrow." Kate smiled again. "I'll be home every night."

Marnie's face brightened, only then to dim. "That'd be great, but it's just too risky. I'd hate to put you in danger."

Kate got to her feet. "Don't worry about that. I'm not. Look, I hate to leave, but I'm due to fly out shortly. Are you sure you'll be okay?"

Marnie put up a brave front. "I'll be fine. This place is crawling with FBI."

"Tell me about it," Kate said. "I thought I was going to have to go back home and get my birth certificate in order to get past them."

Marnie laughed. "You're just the tonic I needed, my friend."

Kate's face turned serious. "You sure you'll be okay?"

"I'll be fine. I promise."

Marnie heard the clock chime ten. Still Tate had not come home.

After Kate had left, Marnie had visited with Annie over a light dinner. Then, a cup of coffee in hand, she'd gone into the den where she'd sat, thumbing through one magazine after another. Finally she had gone to her room—to bed but not to sleep.

Marnie knew it was foolish to worry about Tate, but she couldn't help it. What if... No, she wouldn't think about that possibility. She was crazy enough just thinking about Lance and what he was going through. She didn't intend to add Tate to her list. Anyway, she knew he could take care of himself. In his present mood she pitied anyone who crossed him, herself included.

Suddenly disgusted with her thoughts, Marnie tossed back the cover and got out of bed.

"What you need is some hot chocolate," she muttered aloud.

A short time later, having consumed a cup of hot chocolate milk, she walked out the door to the kitchen, only to suddenly come to a halt. Tate was standing in the shadowy hallway, only a hairbreadth away.

"Oh," she mouthed, stunned.

His lips parted as if to speak, but nothing came out.

Suddenly fear consumed Marnie. "It's Lance, isn't it?" she whispered, clutching at him. "Something's happened to Lance."

At the unexpected sight of her, Tate wanted to run—disappear; instead he felt as if he were trapped between walls of cement.

Yet he was aware of the chiming of the small grandfather clock and the soft glow of the light left burning in the kitchen. He was aware of Marnie staring up at him out of those bottomless eyes, wide with fear. But more than that, he was aware she was touching him.

Swallowing hard, he said, "There's been no word on Lance."

"When I saw your face... I thought..." Marnie's words faded, though she still didn't move. Nor did her hand. It stayed firmly on his chest. The touch was like magic.

It affected his body as if he'd been buried inside her in a hot, withering embrace. He felt his flesh stiffen, and he winced.

"Tate?" She still sounded frightened. Her mouth was trembling, yet so soft, so kissable.

He forced himself to say something, anything. "I didn't mean to scare you."

"That's all right," she whispered.

The light behind her cast her in an ethereal glow. He could smell her hair; it reminded him of the fresh spring rain that had so recently fallen. It adhered in wisps to her cheeks, giving her a wild, tousled look.

Slowly his eyes moved over her body, lingering on the gentle swell of her breasts, the nipples visible through the thin material of her robe. They were pointed, as if begging to be stroked.

The heat rose quickly to his skin, and her hand moved on his chest, lightly like a caress. Instantly he was trapped again, trapped by his body, bound by a liquid heat surging through him.

God! How can you think about sex when your son—

"Tate?"

The strangled use of his name shattered the spell. He dropped his hands suddenly as if he'd touched a furnace and stepped back.

They remained silent for long, heavy seconds.

"What are you doing up?" he asked, sucking much-needed air through his lungs.

"I . . . couldn't sleep."

"Still thinking about your place?"

Marnie drew an unsteady breath. "Yes."

"No one can get to you here. This place is like a fortress."

"I know I keep asking this, but is—is this nightmare ever going to end?"

"I don't know," he said bleakly, "I honestly don't know." He turned away and stared down the dark empty hall. "If only the bastards would call."

"We're . . . you're at their mercy. All you can do is wait."

"Yeah, and that's something I don't do very well."

"I . . . know."

She moved then, and he caught another whiff of her scent. He inhaled deeply, determined to fill his lungs with it.

He knew then that if he didn't leave this second, he wouldn't leave at all. She looked so vulnerable, so frail, as if a gentle breeze could blow her away. The urge was so strong to pull her into his arms, to kiss her until she melted against him and begged for more, that it made him sick to his stomach.

"You'd better go back to bed," he said abruptly, "before you fall on your face."

"The same could be said for you." Her voice, husky and soft, flowed through him like rare, soothing wine.

"It's been a helluva day."

She nodded. Their eyes met.

He could see the steady beat of a vein at her temple. She swallowed noticeably, then backed away. "Good . . . night," she whispered.

She was halfway down the hall when he stopped her. "Marnie."

She turned around.

"Are . . . are you in love with my son?"

He heard her sharp intake of breath and knew she was shocked by his question. He cursed silently while she looked at him long and hard, her features seemingly frozen. Then, without answering, she turned and walked away.

The moment he heard her door shut, he leaned against the wall, feeling what little energy he had left seep out of him as if it was his own blood.

What had she done to him? He wondered if he'd ever get her off the brain. She had truly bewitched him, arousing sensations in him that he had not experienced in years. This lady, his conscience kept saying, he could hurt. And she could hurt him. Either way, it was wrong. Dead wrong.

"You must be Marnie."

Marnie smiled at the woman walking toward her. Clearly in her seventies, she was thin and fragile looking, though her still-lovely face was etched with strength.

"And you must be Mrs. O'Brien," Marnie said, extending her hand.

She clasped Marnie's hand warmly. "Please, call me Edith."

"Edith, it is," Marnie said lightly. She had been curious about Tate's mother, but as yet had never had the pleasure of meeting her. She wished now it wasn't under such painful and trying circumstances.

Still, Marnie was glad of the break in her routine. Since that incident with Tate in the hallway, two days had passed. Except for the few hours she'd spent at her condo supervising its restoration, she'd been at loose ends. Hours had been spent by the pool, soaking up the healing sunshine. Today was no exception.

After breakfast, she'd wandered outside and had been here ever since. It would soon be lunchtime. Tomorrow, thank goodness, she was returning to work. Just yesterday the doctor had deemed her fit to once again assume her responsibilities.

In the meantime, however, a visit from this soft-spoken woman gave Marnie's spirits the lift they needed.

Yet Edith was anything but cheerful. Marnie didn't have to be told that she had aged since her grandson had been kidnapped. Though she was smiling, her eyes were filled with a deep sadness.

"I thought I might actually catch Tate before he left," she said, sitting in the cushioned chair opposite Marnie, "but Annie told me I was too late."

Marnie pushed her sunglasses closer to the bridge of her nose. "He's been going to the office early every morning. Since Lance—" Marnie broke off, watching as Edith's face whitened.

"Poor Tate," Edith said after a moment, her eyes swimming with tears. "This has been so hard on him."

"It's been hard on everyone," Marnie said softly.

"I know, but somehow Tate thinks it was his fault." Without looking directly at Marnie, she went on, "You know they had their differences before he . . . he disappeared."

Marnie sighed. "I—I know."

A silence fell between them.

"My grandson is right," Edith said unexpectedly. "You are beautiful."

Marnie squirmed in her chair. "Thank . . . you."

"Are you surprised he confided in me?"

"I guess I am."

"My grandson told me all about you."

"*All?*"

"He told me he was going to marry you but that Tate was adamantly against it."

An intense blush scalded Marnie's face. "Mrs. O'Brien—"

"Edith," she interrupted gently.

Marnie smiled ruefully. "Sorry."

"Look, I'm the one who should be saying I'm sorry," Edith said, leaning forward, her tone gentle. "I know I'm prying where I shouldn't, but it helps to talk about...about Lance." Fresh tears glistened in her eyes and she drew an unsteady breath. "Right now Tate and I aren't able to comfort each other, we're both so broken up."

Marnie tried to swallow the lump that rose to the back of her throat, surprised that she, too, was close to tears. She had thought she had no more tears left to cry. "If only I could remember what the man looked like—"

"Don't, my dear," Edith admonished. "Don't torment yourself. It's something you can't help. After all, you've been through hell yourself."

Try telling your son that, Marnie agonized silently. Aloud, she said, "I know, but still..."

Edith reached over and squeezed her hand. "Just keep the faith. Now, if you'll excuse me," she added, "I have an appointment. But I'll look forward to seeing you again soon."

"Same here," Marnie said with a smile.

Once she was alone again, she closed her eyes and tried not to think.

The phone became the enemy.

A week passed and no phone call. No message. No word whatsoever from the kidnappers.

Marnie made an effort to resume a normal work schedule, but it was impossible. Plainclothesmen lurked about the premises, reminding everyone just how dangerous the situation was.

Tate was in and out of the office, reminding *her* of how dangerous the situation was. Each time their eyes met, accidentally or otherwise, her pulse quickened. However, it was obvious nothing had changed between them.

He still didn't trust her and made a point not to be alone with her, especially at the ranch. She would concede the waiting was tough and that it had taken its toll on him; it had on her, too. But she hadn't behaved like a wounded animal, snapping the head off of anyone who got close to her.

In the evenings he almost never came home until late, long after she was in bed. On the two occasions he'd parted from that ritual, they had barely been civil to each other through dinner. Then he had politely excused himself and gone to his office.

But this evening she would fool him. She wouldn't be in bed. Earlier, after having returned from the nursing home—the FBI in tow—she had showered, slipped into a comfortable cotton jumpsuit and made her way into the den.

After grabbing a magazine, she had eased down onto the couch, switched on the lamp beside it and curled her bare feet under her. She knew that she must have fallen asleep because she didn't hear him until he called her name.

"Marnie?"

For a moment she sat in a confused fog. Then on unsteady feet, she stood. "Tate?"

"Who else?"

"I—I must have fallen asleep," she said, offering a hapless, halfhearted smile.

His deep stride brought him within touching distance of her.

She automatically stepped back and turned away, his closeness an all-out assault on her senses.

"Why are you still up?"

"What—what time is it?"

"Nearly midnight."

She ran a hand through her already tousled curls. She knew she must look a mess, but she didn't care.

"You should be in bed." His voice sounded rusty.

"So should you," she whispered, looking up at him now, at his pale, haggard face. He was once again dressed in faded jeans and a casual shirt, the top buttons undone to reveal a mat of wiry, dark hair.

Consciously lowering her head, Marnie gave in to the tingling sensation that ran up and down her spine, and wondered if her body trembled from the cool breeze blowing through the open French doors or from his hypnotic power.

Quickly, she jerked her face up, and when she did, her startled eyes collided with his.

"I think you'd best tell me what this is all about," he said roughly.

"I'd like to talk to you."

"Now?"

"Yes, now."

"What about?" He dragged the back of his hand across his mustache.

"I'm leaving."

He blinked. "You're what?"

"I'm leaving," she repeated, drawing a pattern across her lower lip with her tongue. "I...can't—I won't stay here any longer. It's obvious you not only blame yourself for what happened to Lance, but me, as well."

"You damn right I do," he lashed out.

A silent scream of denial caught in her throat.

"But that's beside the point," he added, his tone low and less abrasive.

Marnie clenched and unclenched her fingers. "It is not beside the point. It *is* the point."

They glared at each other.

"It's—it's insane to—to blame me," she finally whispered.

He turned away, closed his eyes and exhaled sharply. "If he hadn't been so smitten with you, he might have been more alert, more on guard."

Marnie almost strangled on her own fury. "That's the most ridiculous thing I've ever heard, and you know it. And that's the reason I'm leaving. Tomorrow. I'm going to Kate's."

"Like hell you are. You're not going anyplace."

"I don't have to answer to you! You're not my keeper. Or my jailer."

"You damn well have to answer to the authorities. They won't let you leave. Count on that."

He was right, of course, Marnie reasoned with a sinking heart. She was trapped, but she sure didn't have to like it. Her thoughts raging, she spun around and took a step.

"Oh, no you don't," he said, latching on to her arms and hauling her against his chest. "Until my son is found, you'll do exactly as you're told."

Marnie stared down at his hands digging into her arms like clamps, then back up to his face. The color ran from her face, and their breaths mingled.

Later, Marnie couldn't say when the mood changed. Suddenly breathing became an effort as she stared at Tate. Her heart rose into her throat.

Move... now. Now.... Now!

The command was urgent, but her body seemed made of lead. Only her rapid, shallow breathing proved that she was still alive.

"Marnie, oh, Marnie." Tate's voice sounded as if it had been dug out of him.

"Tate... please."

His lips, when they touched hers, were hot and hard. She clutched at him frantically as his tongue, soft and insistent, meshed with hers.

"Oh, Marnie," he groaned again, unzipping the front of her jumpsuit. When her breasts spilled into his hands, she groaned.

His kiss hardened while he tugged on a nipple, as if trying to draw the very life from it.

Then suddenly it was over as quickly as it had begun. With tormented eyes and a deep groan, he thrust her away from him.

"Marnie...I—" Tate began in a thick voice.

"Don't," she cried, backing up, her eyes on fire with tears. "Don't you dare say another word."

With that she turned and fled.

Seven

———

Tate dreaded going to bed, knowing he wouldn't sleep. But his body didn't seem to care; it cried for rest. Not only had he put in long hours at the plant, he had also put in long hours at the stables. Back-breaking physical work had been his stress management. But even that had its limit.

Now, stretched on the bed, he clasped his hands behind his head and fixed his eyes on the ceiling. As predicted, he was too wired to sleep. Worry played havoc with his stomach.

Why the hell hadn't the kidnappers called with their demands? It was well over a week now since they had snatched Lance from the city street. He knew the FBI was doing everything it could, but it had come up empty-handed.

His own efforts had also fallen short. He'd ordered Neal to hire the best private detectives in the state. Nothing. It seemed as if Lance had vanished. Gut instinct told him that since the kidnappers had delayed so long, the explosive was not the reason.

If only Marnie could remember what the man looked like. If only Marnie weren't involved in this mess. If only Marnie hadn't come into his life. If....

He flopped onto his side and closed his eyes, hoping to blot thoughts of Marnie from his mind. But Marnie's pale, stricken face wouldn't disappear. He knew she was right; it was ludicrous to blame her. It was equally as ludicrous to blame himself. But he did.

Suddenly he wondered if he would ever be free of guilt. Or was it something that attached itself to a person and never let go?

He had purposefully not wanted to think about Marnie or the hot, torrid kiss they had exchanged only a short while ago. Ah, but she'd felt so good in his arms, so right. Every detail was imprinted on his brain—the brush of her hair like silk against his cheek, the quivering softness of her lips, the feel of her hands on his skin.

Clenching his eyes shut, he groaned as he felt his body respond.

Without warning, Marnie had become his lifeblood and cross.

Maybe he should let her leave. Maybe he would. He'd think about that . . . later.

* * *

Marnie paused a few feet from the door of the main office. "Mr. Anderson, is there something I can help you with?"

Sam Anderson, the tall, lanky head custodian, jerked his head up and stared at Marnie through narrow, lazy eyes.

"No, ma'am," he drawled. "I was just checking the bolt on this door. Mr. O'Brien's orders. Said it wasn't working right."

"Well, is it working right now?" she asked pointedly. She had never liked this man, had never liked his insolent attitude. Maybe it was because he seemed to think he was too good for the job.

"Yes, ma'am," he replied, his eyes roaming over her. "It's fixed."

"Good, then I'm sure you have other duties to attend to."

"Yes, ma'am." His grin was bold. "Sure do."

Marnie held herself erect and watched until he sauntered down the hall, then resumed her steps, a troubled frown on her face. She was certain Anderson's ear had been pressed against the door. But why? Curiosity? That was it, of course, she told herself quickly. Since Lance's abduction, emotions around the office, around the entire plant, were running high.

Dismissing the incident from her mind, Marnie walked the remaining distance to the main office. When she reached the spot where the custodian had been standing, she paused and listened. As expected, she heard voices. Tate's voice in particular. Noticing that her hand trembled slightly, she gripped the knob harder and squared her shoulders.

She had bargained on not having to see him this morning. Even so, she had tried to remove all traces of her sleepless night, but she knew she hadn't been successful. The last thing she'd done before she'd left her room was to look at herself in the mirror.

Although her khaki-striped camp dress flattered her figure and was perfect for the lovely spring day and although her hair framed her face perfectly, there was nothing else perfect about her. Her eyes were huge in her thinly drawn face, and the circles were dark and deep. Her makeup did little to hide them or the sad curve of her mouth.

While she was deeply concerned for Lance, she was concerned for herself, as well. Tate had become an obsession. And last night—heat scalded her cheeks—well, that didn't bear thinking about. But think about it she did, about the wanton way she had behaved, about the way her tongue had twined with his greedily, about the way her hands had reached under his shirt and clutched the flesh of his back, about the way she had let his fingers caress her breasts until she was ready to explode inside.

She'd wanted him then. And, God help her, she wanted him now.

Finally, with less control than she would have liked, Marnie took another deep breath and opened the door. The minute she stepped across the threshold, she took one look at Tate and stopped cold.

He was on the phone, listening, his face devoid of color. Without being told, she knew the kidnappers were on the other end of the line.

The long-awaited call had finally come.

Quickly, her eyes scanned the room, locating Stan Courtney standing reed straight to the right of Tate's desk and Mike James on the other side, standing equally erect.

The tension was tangible.

Stan Courtney looked at her and placed a finger against his lips. He need not have worried about her saying anything; she couldn't have uttered a word if she'd had to. She was too caught up in watching Tate, and her heart ached for him.

"I'm Tate O'Brien," he was saying, his tone clear but cold.

He listened, then said, "Dammit, I want to talk to my son."

Marnie's hand went to her throat.

Tate listened again, then suddenly, furiously, he slammed the receiver down on the hook. "The son of a bitch wouldn't tell me what they wanted, said they'd call back later with their demands and a meeting place."

"Damn!" Stan muttered, his lips white and pencil thin.

Mike rubbed the back of his neck. "I second that."

Only Marnie and Tate had nothing to say. From across the room their eyes met in silent horror.

* * *

Marnie had no intention of exploring any farther than the main barn. When she'd first started meandering through the grounds, she'd had no intention of going into the barn at all. She had intended to remain in the open air, hoping that it would soothe her troubled mind.

It had been two days since Tate had received the call, and she had made it a point to stay out of his way. He was more of a bear to be around than ever. Fear of confronting him had chased her outdoors.

But now that she had walked into the barn, she was both curious and awed. She'd known that Tate was a powerful and wealthy man with a passion for quarter horses, but she'd had no idea of the magnitude of his operation.

Once she ventured out of the barn, well-fortified with grain and hay, she wandered down a paved walkway that was lined on each side with stalls.

She paused midway and looked around. Though the first few stalls were empty, she knew she'd stumbled upon Tate's stable of quarter horses. To bear this out, the scent of horseflesh reached her, followed by a loud whinny.

All told there were between fifteen and twenty cement-block stalls with thick plywood walls and wood shavings on the floor. She remained where she was a moment longer, content just to look. Then she moved on, not stopping until she reached an occupied one. There she paused and rubbed a mare's nose.

Though she didn't know much about horses, she had always admired them, thinking them strong, friendly creatures. She had just laid her forehead down on the muzzle of the bay horse when she heard the voice behind her.

"Well, what do you think?"

Marnie swung around.

Tate was leaning against the door, watching her, though his eyes were somewhat shielded by the Stetson angled down over his forehead.

"How come you're up so early?" he asked when she didn't answer.

Marnie swallowed with difficulty, thinking how good he looked in an open-necked shirt and worn, tight jeans. "I thought the fresh air would do me good," she said, her voice quavering slightly.

"Did it do the trick? The fresh air, I mean?"

Her smile was nervous. "Yes," she said, continuing to rub the horse.

Tate moved toward her. "You a horse lover?"

"Yes, only I don't know a lot about them."

For a second he didn't respond, his eyes settling on the gentle swell of her breasts, which were obvious under the thin red T-shirt tucked inside her jeans.

Instantly, her stomach knotted as a spurt of fire darted through her.

"You don't have to know a lot about them to like them." His voice had all the roughness of sandpaper.

"Are—are all your horses quarter horses?" she asked, desperate to break the spell, the same kind of spell that had held them in its grip last night.

"Running quarters, to be exact," he said, his voice not yet back to normal.

"I don't understand."

"They're one-third thoroughbred, which makes them faster."

"Well, whatever. All I know is that they are beautiful with their barrel chests and big hips."

"Ever ridden much?"

"No, no I haven't. Very little, in fact."

"Wanna give it a try?"

Stunned, Marnie sought to catch his eyes, but he kept them fixed on the animal. Silence stretched between them.

"When?" she asked, sounding choked.

"What's wrong with right now?"

"Oh, I don't know. I . . ."

His eyes burned into hers. "If I promise to keep my hands to myself, will you come?"

She caught her breath.

"I won't apologize for the other night," he said roughly.

The stark desire in his eyes made her mouth go dry. "I . . . don't want you to."

They looked at each other for another long moment, then Tate asked in a low tone, "Well, are you game?"

Marnie slid a glance at the mare. "What if I fall off?"

Suddenly he threw back his head and laughed. "We'll cross that bridge when we come to it, okay?"

She had never heard him laugh before, not a deep belly laugh like now. It sent her blood pulsing through her veins like warm, heady brandy.

"Okay," she said on a breathy sigh.

It took them a half hour to cross the open pasture into the edge of the thicket that was also part of Tate's land. But it wasn't because Marnie was having trouble managing her mare; she wasn't. They got along supremely well, and she was proud of herself. It was because there had been so much to see that she had wanted to take her time, soak up the beautiful surroundings.

Marnie and Tate paused under a huge oak and faced each other. Marnie was the first to speak.

"This is heavenly. I can see why you're addicted."

He quirked an eyebrow. "So you know that I'm horse crazy, huh?"

"Lance told me," she said hesitantly.

"What else did Lance tell you?" He paused deliberately and looked at her with smiling eyes. "About me, that is?"

"Not—not much."

Amusement curved his full lips. "Liar."

Marnie colored and tried not to show her surprise at Tate's sudden change in mood. This was a side of him she had never seen before, and she was loath to say or do anything that would cause him to revert to his cold, cynical self.

"Come on, fess up. What did he say?"

Tate O'Brien, teasing her? Unheard of. Still, a potent excitement percolated through her as she stared at him, a smile softening her lips. "Mostly that your bark's much worse than your bite."

"And do you agree?"

An abrupt tension swept away all humor.

"I don't know," she finally said, the words coming out in a rush.

An impatience came and went in his eyes. "What's important to you, Marnie Lee?" he asked, changing the subject. "What do you want out of life?"

"A job that I find challenging and enough money to live comfortably."

"In that order?"

"No, actually money comes first," she said honestly, and waited for the fireworks.

None came. Instead he asked in a benign voice, "Because of your father?"

She stared at him, perplexed. "How'd you know...?" Her voice trailed off, and her features changed. "I'd forgotten you know everything there is to know about me," she said, disconcerted.

"Not everything."

It wasn't so much what he said that sent a tremor through her, but the way he said it.

"Oh, and just exactly what is it you don't know?"

"How you really feel about my son." His gaze never flickered. With maddening slowness his eyes wandered over her. "You never answered that question."

His voice was once again a husky, seductive lure, and she felt herself responding.

"I want an answer—now."

She circled her dry lips with her tongue. "I care about him, but I—I don't love him."

"Thanks for being honest." His face betrayed no emotion, but a muscle twitched in his jaw.

"He'll...be all right." Her voice broke. "He just has to be."

Tate toyed with the brim of his hat. "God, I hope you're right."

"And I want you to know that I haven't given up hope of regaining my memory," she whispered, her voice as dry as a rustling leaf.

His eyes held hers for a long moment, revealing nothing. Then he said brusquely, "Come on, let's ride."

Again they rode in silence in and out of the thicket, not stopping until they reached a clearing. They sat atop their mounts and watched the sunset.

"Tate."

"Mmm," he murmured without looking at her.

"I'm not sure this means anything, but I caught Anderson..."

It happened then. One gunshot. Then another. Then another. All were close. Too close.

"What...!" Tate got no further as another bullet passed by Marnie's head.

Her horse bolted. "Tate!" she screamed, struggling to hold on.

White-lipped, Tate reached for the reins, but it was too late.

Suddenly the mare pitched Marnie, tossing her on the ground like a broken, discarded rag doll.

"Oh, God," Tate wheezed, clearing his mount and scrambling to her, cradling her in his arms. "Marnie, talk to me!"

Marnie knew she wasn't dead. Or at least she didn't think so. But she was stiff enough to be dead, she told herself, wincing. With her eyes closed, she wiggled one toe, then another. So far so good.

What was wrong? Why did she feel as if she were trying to swim to the surface while currents pulled her under? She opened her eyes and moved them carefully across the ceiling, then around the room. Where was she?

Moonlight, spilling through the window, cast the room in shadows. She moved again and this time felt nothing but relief; it didn't hurt.

Suddenly, with the impact of a blow to the head, she remembered. Gun shots. Someone had tried to kill her.

"Oh," she whimpered aloud, trying to swallow around the golf-ball sized lump in her throat. She couldn't. It refused to dissolve. In order to keep from strangling, Marnie let the hot tears flow.

"Oh, no. . . ." she whimpered again. Had Tate been hurt? Had the bullets struck him instead of her?

Frantically, her mind groped to bring the entire scenario into focus. Tate couldn't have been hit because he had come to her rescue. A giddy feeling of relief replaced her panic.

She could see Tate, white-lipped and shaking, bending over her, cradling her hand on his knee, hear him cry.

"Tate," she breathed, fully conscious but dazed.

"Thank God." He'd looked up then, as if delivering a prayer of thanks. Without saying anything else, he ran his hand over her body.

"The bullet missed me...but my head is pounding." She placed a hand on her head. "What about you? Are—are you all right?"

"I'm fine," he said, his voice biting. "But the son of a bitch who shot at us won't be fine when I'm through with him."

With what energy she could muster, Marnie reached out and clutched at the front of his shirt. "Who—who would do such a thing?"

Tate didn't say anything. Instead his features turned harder and his eyes icier as if he were making a pact with the devil right there on the spot.

The look on his face frightened Marnie more than if he'd lashed out the truth. Her hold on his shirt tightened. "You—you think he...they were shooting at us? At me?"

His jaw clenched. "No more questions. I'm taking you home."

After he'd gently secured her in the saddle in front of him, she remembered very little, only bits and pieces of the following hours.

Now, as she eased to her elbows, Marnie wondered who had put her in bed—naked, except for panties. Tate? The thought weakened her further.

Her heart rate settled; Annie had taken charge. Tate had left her in the housekeeper's competent hands.

She laid her head back but felt no comfort, other than the fact that neither she or Tate was seriously injured.

What she felt was anger, gut-wrenching anger. Suddenly she longed to run away from the nightmare that was now her life, run from the men who were trying to harm her, run from thoughts of Lance. But most of all, she wanted to run from Tate, who with one look, one touch, could make her ache like a woman in love. A familiar surge of dread swelled inside her. She couldn't love him.

Surely she hadn't been that stupid, knowing they had no future. Besides, she was just a game to him. When he finished playing, he would fold his cards and walk away.

Without warning, the room began to spin, and like a puppet whose strings have broken, Marnie's head collapsed against the pillow. Deep, wrenching sobs racked her body.

It was only after her weeping had run its course that she heard a noise. She stiffened. Then, ever so slowly, with her heart in her throat, Marnie shifted back into a sitting position and stared at the door.

As feared, a figure stood on the threshold. She gasped and squeezed the sheet to her breasts.

"Marnie."

"Tate?" Her voice was a mere whisper.

"I—I heard you crying."

She opened her mouth, but speech was impossible. She could only stare at his bare chest and jean-clad hips and tremble.

"Marnie," he whispered again.

Another sob escaped her lips.

"Marnie, don't ... please." His voice sounded broken.

"Oh, Tate," she cried, "I ..." She stopped and watched as he began walking toward her in slow motion. He seemed unaware that his legs were moving.

No! This was insane. If he touched her now ... She had to stop him. She couldn't let him near her, especially not now, not in her weakened condition. She had to be strong.

But with each step he took, that voice of caution dwindled.

He moved closer, and her heart almost stopped beating.

Neither spoke.

Tears marked her face.

"Marnie ... it's all right." He stopped a foot from her.

She stared up at him for long moments, her soul in her eyes.

He needed her. He needed her *now*.

It was an all-consuming need that knew no boundaries. And, for the first time, his feelings for Marnie were not tempered with guilt. His screaming conscience had been completely stifled.

For hours after the shooting incident, Marnie had preyed on his mind. In the end he knew he couldn't settle down until he'd assured himself one more time that she was sleeping soundly.

He'd left his room and walked down the hall to hers. Without hesitation, he had twisted the knob and pushed open the door.

That was as far as he'd gotten.

His muscles had locked. The bright moonlight had perfected his vision, enabling him to see her clearly. One shoulder and one long slender leg had been free of cover. Her skin had shone like satin.

His heart had slammed against his rib cage. He had come apart inside; it was just that simple and just that complicated. For the briefest of moments his conscience had tried to rally, but it had been crushed with callous determination.

Now, as he felt himself drowning in those eyes, he tried one more time to pull back. Apologize for intruding, he told himself, and get the hell out.

The apology stuck in his throat. He couldn't take his eyes off her, off her breasts. They were full and high and porcelain-white. The nipples were small, and in the moonlight they glistened like pink pebbles.

Life filled his manhood.

Marnie moaned, seemed to be throbbing, shivering.

Tate's eyes delved lower, taking in the perfect skin, the narrow waist, flat stomach, navel, coming to rest on the top of her panties. The saliva in his mouth dried, and in his mind he was already dispensing with the fragile garment.

The light lingered on her eyes, making them sparkle like violets covered with drops of dew. He wanted to disappear inside her, but contented himself with merely looking at her and saying nothing.

She returned his stare and whispered something incoherent.

Finally, he reached out and ran a thumb across her lips—so like silk. They quivered.

"Marnie..."

Wordlessly, she held out her arms.

"Marnie, oh, Marnie," he muttered, sitting on the bed and slipping into them. "I—I shouldn't be here."

Her fingers sank into his shoulders.

"Please...don't leave me." Her cheeks were smudged with tears.

Tate groaned. Then unable to help himself, he kissed the tears from her face, tears that mingled with his own. Then he gently pushed her to arm's length, struggling for control. "Don't you understand," he cried, facing her again, "I can't just hold you. I—"

She raised a finger to his lips, hushing him. "I know," she whispered. "And it's all right."

"You mean...?"

This time she stopped his flow of words with her lips. Their bare chests touched, and he almost exploded. Blood stampeded through him, settling in his manhood. He stood and quickly discarded his jeans.

"Tate, Tate, Tate." Her tone was agony as she reached for him again and clutched him hard. Then, as if surprised to feel his hardness pressed against her stomach, she gasped.

"See what you do to me," he said thickly, holding her close once again.

They plummeted onto the bed, and in a fluid movement he rolled on top of her, positioning himself so that he could look into her eyes.

"Kiss me," she pleaded.

"Oh, yes, yes," he groaned against her mouth.

Their tongues meshed in a hot, coiling foreplay, and he began to move his hips against hers. He separated from her mouth and raised his head to again watch her face. At the rapture he saw there, all coherent thought fled. She was his, his alone.

He shifted his position, eager to gain access to her breasts while continually brushing the apex of her thighs with his strength.

She gasped again with pleasure and held him close. "You're making me crazy."

After a moment, Tate stopped, disentangled himself and stood beside the bed.

Marnie's eyes widened anxiously.

"Soon, my darling, soon," he whispered, removing her panties.

With both now free of clothing, Marnie reached for him again and opened her legs as he covered her.

"Oh, Marnie..." His groan ended in a cry as he felt her soft hand surround him.

With another muted cry, he slipped deep inside her. She was tight and he tried to hold back, but she wouldn't let him. She locked her legs around his buttocks, and instantly blind urgency claimed them.

"Marnie..." He was unable to say more. He could only feel, feel as he'd never felt before.

She moaned and clung to him.

"Marnie, Marnie.... Oh, Marnie...I want you!" The words were delivered in pulsating gasps, coming from his lips at the same time his warm seed spilled into her. Sweet pain shook their bodies.

"Oh, Tate," she cried.

I love you! God, I love you Marnie! I love you.

Eight

Marnie shifted slightly. Not only was Tate's head on her pillow, but his leg was draped over one of hers, binding them together. She feared any unexpected movement would awaken him and she didn't want to do that. She knew he needed sleep as badly, if not worse than she.

But for now sleep was the furthest thing from her mind. She was far too keyed up. Rather than sleep, she wanted to remember, to savor every moment of their passion.

She let out a quiet, forlorn sigh. She couldn't quite get past the idea that she had somehow betrayed Lance. Still, if she had it to do over again, she wouldn't change a thing. She had known Tate would be a marvelous lover, and he had more than fulfilled her dreams.

What about her? Had she done the same for him? She wanted the answer to be yes so badly it hurt. Yet, she was scared it meant nothing sacred to him, that the passion that forced them to turn to each other time and time again during the night was just that and nothing more.

But hadn't he said he wanted her? Wasn't that a sign he cared? Not necessarily. He had probably told countless women that same thing.

So, in the cold face of midnight, she forced herself to brave reality no matter how much it hurt. She'd seen the fear in his eyes. There had been no mistaking it. It had been heavily camouflaged with passion and lust, but it had been there.

Swallowing her sigh, Marnie stole another glance at him, longing to touch him, if for no other reason than to make sure he was real.

But there *was* another reason. Somewhere along the way, she had indeed lost her way and done the most foolish thing imaginable. She had fallen in love, fallen deeply and irrevocably in love with Tate O'Brien.

And while there was intense joy within her, there was also sadness and fear. Because she loved him, she was at his mercy. With his mouth, his hands, his body, he could manipulate her, control her.

And Dear Lord, she didn't want him to release her, either. It had been so good to be filled, so right to be needed, so exciting to be burdened with his weight.

She didn't want it to end. She didn't want to live apart from this man. Not now. Not ever.

Marnie's eyes moved from his face to the rise and fall of his chest. Finally, for her ears alone, she whispered tearfully, "I love you."

For now that was all her heart could spare.

"Are you asleep?"

"No," Marnie whispered, snuggling closer to Tate's hard, warm body. "Are you?"

He caressed her back with a calloused hand. "No."

"What time is it?" Marnie asked, barely able to speak. His touch was doing strange things to her body.

"Six o'clock."

She groaned.

"I second that."

"Do we have to get up?"

He chuckled, still strumming his fingers across her back. "Not if you don't want to."

"I've been awake since midnight."

Tate moved slightly so that he could peer down at her. "You were thinking." It wasn't a question.

"Yes. About us. About you."

She felt him stiffen. "Go on."

She toyed with the crisp hair on his chest. "Actually, I was thinking about your... wife."

"What about her?" Tate's tone was taut.

Marnie knew she was treading on dangerous ground. "Were...you happily married?" She held her breath.

"No," he said bluntly. "Believe it or not, she always wanted more than I could give her."

The angry pain festering inside him sounded in his voice. Marnie ached for him.

"How did she die?"

"An accident. She'd been drinking and lost control of the car."

"How tragic."

Silence fell between them.

"What about you?" Tate's voice was as warm now as the hand covering her breast. "It's time you fessed up."

Marnie smiled. "I'm afraid I have very little to 'fess up' to."

"Ever been in love?"

Her smile slipped, then completely disappeared. "No."

"I find that hard to believe."

Marnie shifted in his arms. "Well...I thought I was once."

"What happened?"

"I found out he was married with a family."

Tate hesitated, then said, "There's been no one else?"

"No one."

They fell silent again.

Marnie's shuddering breath broke it. "About us...about last night..."

"What do you want me to say, that I'm sorry?"

I want you to say that you love me. "Are . . . you sorry?" she whispered.

"God no. But I didn't mean to touch you," he added in a strained voice.

"I know," she said huskily. "I didn't mean for you to, either."

Tate tipped her chin so that she was forced to look into his eyes. They were troubled. "Are you saying that *you're* sorry?"

She lowered her long, curling lashes. "No."

"Even if you get pregnant?"

Her heart missed a beat. "It's—it's the wrong time of the month."

"Did I hurt you?"

She swallowed. "No."

"It's a wonder. You're so small, so tight. . . ."

"You didn't hurt me." Her voice was husky. "It was wonderful."

"Oh, Marnie, Marnie, what am I going to do with you?"

"What do you want to do?" She hated herself for asking, but she had to.

"I'd like to hole up somewhere and make love to you until we're both so weak we can't move."

"Oh, Tate," she whispered.

"But we both know that's impossible, don't we?"

Her heart sank. Guilt stood like a steel wall between them. And the fact that he didn't love her—she mustn't forget that.

"Yes," she said in a small voice, "I know."

They didn't say anything for a long while, content to simply hold each other.

Finally Marnie asked, "What about the gunshots? Did you find out anything?"

"Not a lot, but I will." His voice was hard. "After I left Annie clucking over you, I called the FBI. Then I went back and looked around."

"And?"

"I found a deserted campsite and two cigarette butts which forensic took in for analysis."

"Do—do you think it's related to—"

"I don't know," he said, interrupting her. "But one thing I do know, there's going to be hell to pay when I get my hands on whoever was behind that little fiasco. If they had hurt you . . ."

His concern brought tears to her eyes. "But they didn't, and that's what counts."

"Yeah, but it was too close a call to suit me."

"This may not mean anything, but remember before we heard the shots, I was telling you about Sam Anderson?"

Tate nodded.

"Well, I was coming down the hall and he was at the office door pretending to work on the lock, only I know he wasn't. He had his ear to the door and was listening in on the conversation between you and the FBI."

Tate frowned. "Why?"

"Curiosity is the only thing I can think of."

His frown deepened. "I don't know. There has to be more to it than that. I'll pass the word on to the FBI and let them look into it." He paused and stared deeply into her eyes. "In the meantime there's something else I want to do."

"And what's that?"

"Make love to you."

A flush stained Marnie's cheeks. Heat spread between her legs. "That's what I want, too."

While sunlight seeped through the windows and the dawn turned into day, Tate reached for her. Her body was warm, ready. He stroked her slowly, gently, creating an ache within her that only his being inside her would alleviate.

When he lifted her on top and eased her down on him, her lips parted wildly and her eyes rolled back.

"Ah...Tate," she moaned, giving in to the sensations racking her body. He filled her completely.

"Easy does it, baby."

Splaying his hands across her back, he eased her forward and took a nipple in his mouth. As he sucked on it like a greedy child, she moaned again and together they began to move.

Afterward, with him still inside her, she collapsed on his sweat-riddled chest. She was still there a few minutes later when the phone rang.

Instantly alert, Tate eased her away and reached for the receiver.

"Hello," he said, his tone short.

Equally alert, Marnie watched, suddenly uneasy.

Tate held the phone out to her. "For you—it's the nursing home."

Doing her best not to panic, she took the receiver. "This is Marnie Lee."

Moments later the receiver slipped from her hand. Her face was stark white. "It's ... Daddy—he's disappeared."

"Where can he be?" Marnie asked on a wail.

"Trust me," Tate said, "it's going to be all right. We'll find him. How can we miss with the police, the FBI and us looking for him?"

Marnie sighed and rubbed her temple. She wished she could be as self-confident about finding Silas as Tate was.

Since the call had roused them out of bed, events had passed in a haze for Marnie, reminding her of the night Lance was kidnapped. After Tate had hung up the phone for her, he'd drawn her close against him and held her.

Her first thought, of course, was that Silas had been kidnapped in retaliation.

"Now, now," Tate had consoled as if reading her mind, "let's not jump to conclusions until we have all the facts."

Everything else forgotten, they had quickly made their way to the home, where they had been met by the administrator and head nurse. Both had informed Marnie that one minute Mr. Lee was sitting on the porch and the next he wasn't.

"How could he just disappear?" Marnie had demanded, looking from one to the other.

"Unfortunately, we don't have an answer for you, Ms. Lee," the administrator had said in an embarrassed tone.

Two hours later Silas had still not been found. It was as if he had disappeared into thin air—or worse, into the kidnappers' hands.

Marnie and Tate were now tramping through the woods beyond the home's lawn, thinking that Silas might have wandered there. But with each step, with each minute, Marnie's fear increased along with her frustration.

Cutting a glance at Tate, she knew that he felt the same way, in spite of his earlier words to the contrary. Worry lines now ruled his forehead.

"I...do you think they took him because—because of me?"

Tate stopped and faced her, only he didn't say anything. Instead, he touched her cheek with his finger, purposely trapping a lone tear that was trickling down her cheek and threatening to land on her blouse.

"Oh, honey," he said, "I don't think it's like that at all, though I won't say I'm not concerned. And certainly your fears could turn out to be reality, but I don't think so."

"I hope and pray you're right."

They resumed walking, and Marnie felt comforted as Tate kept his arm loosely around her shoulders. She reveled in his strength and didn't want to think about what she would have done if he hadn't been there to take charge.

Yet she knew she shouldn't be thinking such thoughts. She shouldn't depend on him. In the end she knew it would only bring her more heartache. But after last night she didn't have either the strength or the desire to put distance between them.

"Ms. Lee!"

They both froze in their tracks, recognizing the excited ring in the voice.

Marnie's eyes widened. "Oh, Tate…" She couldn't go on.

He grabbed her hand. "Let's go."

In order to avoid the undergrowth, they were forced to move more slowly than they would have liked. Even at that, Marnie wasn't prepared when a stray limb slapped her across the upper arm.

"Ouch!" she yelped.

Tate stopped midstride and swung around. "What's wrong?" Concern sharpened his tone.

"Nothing," Marnie managed to say between gulps, the stinging sensation making her sick to her stomach. "I'm all right. A limb just grazed me, that's all. Please, let's hurry."

"Whoa, hold it," Tate warned, clamping a hand down on one shoulder. "If you fall and hurt yourself, what good will you be to your dad?"

Marnie squinted against the bright sunlight. "I know, but I'm still so scared."

"I know," Tate murmured softly. "I know."

Finally they made it through the last clump of trees. Silas Lee, flanked on each side by the nurse and administrator, was standing in the middle of the clearing.

"Thank God," Marnie cried, smiling up at Tate.

With that same finger, Tate touched her cheek tenderly. "Well, what are you waiting for? Go give him a hug."

A short time later Silas was back in his room, sitting in his favorite chair by the window. Marnie stood beside him, while Tate leaned against the wall and eyed them closely.

"How long has he been like this?" he asked.

A sad smile appeared on Marnie's face at the same time her fingers slicked down the cowlick sticking up in the crown of Silas's head. "Forever."

Tate's eyebrows shot up.

Marnie sighed as their eyes met. "That's an exaggeration, of course. I know this sounds awful, but when I try to remember how sharp, how active he was, I can't." Her eyes pleaded with Tate to understand. "When I'm home or at work and try to think about the good times we had, they're murky. All I can see is the way he is now, and it breaks my heart."

Tate's mouth was stretched into a grim line. "I can imagine how tough it must be for you to see someone you love stricken with this blasted disease."

"The worst part of it, he won't get any better. He'll only get worse."

For a moment there was silence. Then Tate asked, "Are you sure he's in the right place?"

"The very best money can buy."

"Then how in the hell did he just wander off?"

Marnie's eyebrows knitted together. How *had* he just wandered off? Silas Lee had done what so many other Alzheimer patients had done; he had simply walked off, lost as if he were a newborn baby. The home staff had been distraught, full of recriminations and apologies. Those, however, had done little to relieve her anxious mind.

As if sensing her torment, Tate reached out with a steady hand and patted her shoulder. When he spoke, his tone was less harsh. "Sorry, I didn't mean to—"

She cut him off. "Don't apologize. You're right. I'm asking myself the same thing."

"I'd feel better if he had round-the-clock protection."

She avoided his gaze. "That goes without saying, only I can't afford it."

"Well, I can," he said flatly.

Marnie's eyes sought his, an incredulous expression in them. "You'd do that for me?"

His gaze didn't waver. "Yes, I'd do that for you."

Marnie licked her lips. "I'll...repay you, of course. Somehow."

"Forget it," he said roughly.

"I—"

"I said forget it."

She decided to do as he said.

"Look, I'm going to the office," Tate said then. "Will you be all right?"

Marnie smiled. "I'll be fine."

"You sure?"

"I'm sure."

He gave her a long, slow look, then moved within a hairbreadth of her. "Call if you need me," he said huskily.

"I . . . will."

He leaned toward her and laid his mouth against hers. Clutching at him, Marnie parted her lips beneath his.

When it was apparent neither one could breathe, Tate pulled away. "Later," he whispered thickly before turning and walking out the door.

Afterward, Marnie lost all concept of time. She had no idea how long she sat beside her daddy, holding his hand, talking to him. But when she finally got up and left, she could still taste Tate's kiss on her lips.

Where the hell was Courtney? Tate wondered with impatience. The agent had called him over an hour before and said he was on his way.

Before now, Tate hadn't had time to get anxious. The second he'd walked into the office, he'd sent for his assistant. Without mincing words, he'd told Neal to see to it that Silas Lee had twenty-four-hour protection.

Once Neal had left to do his bidding, Tate had thumbed through the stack of contracts that Marnie had put on his desk. But he hadn't been able to concentrate. Even the folder stamped in bold letters, CLASSIFIED, hadn't held his attention. Inside it were the final plans of the plastic explosive, plans that the government had approved without a snag.

Lance would be proud.

Oh, God, son, are you still alive?

He glared down at the papers strewn across his desk as if they were his enemies. Suddenly, in a fit of frustration and anger, Tate longed to rid the desk of its contents. He refrained, of course. He had always prided himself on having control of his emotions. Until now he had always had. But with his fear over Lance and his passion for Marnie, his control was being pushed to its limits.

Was he destined to begin and end every day for the rest of his life with thoughts of her? Yes, his heart answered. When he'd touched her last night, a slow burn had started deep within him. And when he'd embedded himself inside her tight softness, that slow burn had raged into an inferno, and the fire was still smoldering inside him.

He had lost control. The last thing he'd planned was to fall in love with the woman his son loved.... No! It wasn't love he felt; it couldn't be. But he knew it was. Only love could tear his soul to pieces, make him wish he were dead when he was in perfect health.

Even now, as he stood, her delicate scent seemed to have settled on his skin. The sweetness of it made him ache. He wanted her. Again. And again.

"O'Brien."

Startled, Tate jerked his head around. Agent Courtney was peeking around the door.

"Come on in," Tate said abruptly, almost rudely. Then he cursed. It wasn't fair to use the agent as his whipping boy.

"I knocked..." Courtney broke off with a shrug. His face was almost as red as his hair.

"Sorry," Tate muttered, "I didn't hear you."

"That's understandable with all you've got on your mind."

"Have a seat," Tate invited. When the agent was settled, Tate asked, "Everything still all right at the home?"

"Was when I left."

"Good," Tate said.

Courtney's eyes narrowed. "But that's not what you wanted to talk about, is it?"

"No." Tate let out a slow breath. "It's about a man by the name of Anderson who works here as the head custodian."

The agent crossed one knee over the other. "What about him?"

"Marnie caught him eavesdropping on our conversation."

"And you think it might be more than curiosity?"

"Don't know, but it wouldn't hurt to check it out." Tate paused and reached for another folder on his desk and then tossed it to the agent. "His personnel file. We checked him out carefully, of course, but we could've missed something that your sophisticated computers can pick up."

"Never can tell. We'll get on it."

A short silence ensued.

"Do you think Lance is still alive?" Tate asked, forcing the words out.

Courtney sighed. "I wish the hell I knew."

"The waiting—that's what's so damned tough."

"I know. And what beats me is they haven't called back with their demands."

Tate rubbed the back of his neck. "That's precisely why my gut instinct tells me it's amateurs that grabbed him."

"With dumb luck on their side."

"Exactly." Tate stood and came from behind his desk. "If it had been terrorists wanting the design, they would have already moved. I think whoever took Lance has an ax to grind either against Lance or me."

"Or the company."

Tate perched on the edge of his desk. "I think they did it for the money."

"So why the delay?"

"That I can't answer."

For a long second the room was hushed.

"Tell me, Courtney," Tate said at last, "do you ever get tired of dealing with the slimeballs of the world?"

"Every day, Mr. O'Brien, every day. And speaking of slimeballs, I guess I'd better check out the one you just gave me."

Tate's lips tightened. "Let me know."

Courtney eased to his feet. "Count on it."

It was late when Marnie maneuvered her car out of the parking lot at the home and headed toward the plant. She'd decided that if Tate's car was there, she would stop and see if there was anything she needed to do.

She wanted to be near him; it was that simple. Silas's sudden disappearance had robbed her of the opportunity to think about their lovemaking last night, but the memory had teased her all day like a brightly wrapped package under the tree that couldn't be opened until Christmas day.

Now as she sped down the boulevard, vivid details raced to the forefront of her mind and she gripped the steering wheel hard to keep from whimpering aloud.

It was then that she saw Sam Anderson walk out of the convenience store across from Systems.

Afterward she had no idea why she bothered to slow down and watch him. At the time she operated purely on instinct. Maybe it was the way his eyes kept shifting from right to left as if he was looking for something or someone.

A small, nondescript car suddenly swept toward the curb and braked. Marnie continued to stare, more out of curiosity than anything else. But ever since she'd caught Anderson eavesdropping, she hadn't trusted him.

The driver, she noted, seemed as nondescript as the car. Yet there was something familiar about him, something she couldn't quite put her finger on. Perhaps he, too, worked at the plant and she'd noticed him in passing.

"You're losing it, Lee," she said aloud, pressing down on the accelerator.

It was only after she reached the plant parking lot that it struck her where she'd seen him.

"Oh, no!" Marnie cried, tearing out of the car. She didn't stop until she reached Tate's office. Without knocking she thrust open the door, out of breath.

Courtney, heading toward the door himself, came to an abrupt halt. Tate's face turned white. "Marnie?"

"I remember what the man looked like." She paused and sucked in a breath. "In fact, I just saw him. He used to work here."

Nine

The sky glittered with stars while the moon hung in their midst like a huge ball of fire in the midnight sky.

As she strolled along the edge of the swimming pool, Marnie raised her head and pulled the fresh air into her lungs. Still looking up, she tried to force herself to relax, to enjoy the beauty of the warm spring night.

She couldn't. No matter how breathtaking, how spectacular the sight was before her, she couldn't lose herself in it. Her insides were coiled as if she'd been punched in the stomach and was expecting another blow.

But then after the day she'd had, how could she expect otherwise? Even now, hours after the fact, she found it hard to believe she'd seen the man who had taken Lance. It had to be one of those quirky twists of fate; there was no other explanation for it.

The instant she had walked into Tate's office and told him and Courtney what she had seen, events had steamrolled. An all-points bulletin was put out on Walter Elliot, a former employee who had recently been fired, and on Anderson, who had not shown up for work during the past few days.

Following another sigh, Marnie stopped and slipped the oversized T-shirt over her head to reveal a bikini underneath. The bathing suit, a seductive burgundy, left very little to the imagination. For a moment she wished Tate could see her in it.

Then chastising herself for such a thought, she sat down on the side of the pool and dunked both feet into the water. Ah, heaven, she thought, feeling the water penetrate her limbs like a soothing balm. Shortly, she lifted her head and looked around, the moon providing her with adequate lighting.

By anyone's standards the haven, which included the deck and pool, was as beautiful as it was peaceful. Marnie's gaze fell on the twelve-foot-high stockade fence that surrounded it, offering the maximum of privacy even from the agents who continuously combed the grounds. Her eyes wandered back to the pool, mesmerized by its kidney-shaped beauty.

No doubt about it, Tate had the best of everything. But she felt no envy, only regret. Regret because she did not fit into his world of glitz and glamour, no matter how hard she might want to.

Suddenly, her eyes turned toward the house and Tate's bedroom. All was dark. She wasn't surprised. In Lance's absence Tate was working long hours.

On the way from the police station, she had asked him if he wanted her to help him clear his desk. He'd said no, insisting she return to the ranch, telling her she'd had enough excitement for one day.

But she hadn't wanted to leave him. The night without him had been dismal; the thought of a future without him was more dismal.

"Is this a private party?"

At the sound of his voice, Marnie nearly jumped out of her skin. Turning rounded eyes on him, she noticed he was standing to her right, clad in a pair of black trunks and nothing else.

"Did I scare you?" Tate asked, sitting down beside her.

"Yes."

"Sorry, didn't mean to."

Her heart was beating fast. "How . . . did you know where I was?"

"I went to your room."

Somewhere close by a cricket chirped. A soft breeze blew, filling the air with the scent of flowers. Neither noticed, so intent were they in each other.

"You—you did," Marnie said inanely, thinking how good he looked, how good he smelled. She couldn't stop thinking about what it felt like to touch him.

"I thought you'd be asleep."

She leveled her gaze on his face. "I tried but I couldn't."

"I'm not surprised. Sleep doesn't come easily to me these days, either."

"Are—are you just getting home from the office?" The minute the question passed her lips, Marnie wished she could recall it. Color stole into her face.

"Sorry," she added before he had a chance to respond. "I didn't mean to pry." Of course, she meant to pry. But what if he gives you an answer you don't want to hear? For all she knew, he could have been making love to his blond friend. The thought made her ill.

"Marnie, look at me."

Swallowing, she faced him.

"You have every right to pry," he said thickly.

"No…"

"Yes." His eyes held her. "Since I met you, I haven't been with another woman."

"Oh, Tate," she whispered, looking at him, enjoying the hard flex of his muscles as he leaned back and braced himself on his elbows. "We've got ourselves in a mess, haven't we?"

"A helluva one," he echoed with a ghost of a smile.

They were quiet for a while.

"Do you think they'll catch Elliot?" Marnie finally asked, kicking the water with one foot.

"It's only a matter of time."

"I hope you're right."

"I know what you're thinking."

"You do?"

"Why Anderson and Elliot would risk being seen together in broad daylight?"

Marnie frowned. "It just doesn't make sense."

"No, it doesn't. But like I said before, you never know about sickos."

"In light of what we know, do you think it was Anderson who was driving the car that night they took Lance?"

"More than likely. And to think that sonofabitch has been working for the company all this time."

"What about Elliot?"

"Him, too, but at least one of the engineers had enough sense to fire him for not doing his work."

"So you think they got together and planned the whole thing? I find that hard to believe."

"Me, too."

"Then it has to be revenge they want instead of money," Marnie said, thinking aloud.

"Exactly."

"Well, all I can say is that you have to be slightly deranged to do something like that."

Tate's face was as hard as his tone. "It's those types who have the guts to do it."

Marnie designed patterns in the water with her feet. "I can hardly stand to think about it. When I saw him today, that whole nightmarish episode replayed itself in my mind until I thought I'd scream."

"Shh, don't think about that now. You're safe." Tate's eyes were dark with concern. "Wanna swim?"

"I'd love to," she said, though a bit shakily.

Tate stood, only to then use the edge as a spring board and split the water with a perfect dive. When his head reappeared, Marnie eased into the pool.

Side by side they swam to the opposite end, but instead of clinging to the side and resting, Tate heaved himself up and out of the water. Startled, Marnie watched as he peeled off his trunks and kicked them aside with a toe.

Her breath hung suspended as the moonlight played over his aroused body.

With his eyes fixed on hers, he got back into the water and placed his hands on her shoulders.

"Every time I'm around you, I want to touch you."

"I feel the same way."

He kissed her then, with no excuses.

"You shouldn't . . . we shouldn't . . ." she whispered at last.

"Why?"

"The agents. They—"

"Can't see us," he murmured against her lips.

"Are you sure?"

"Positive," he said, sliding the flimsy straps off her shoulders, stroking them.

"Mmm, that feels good."

"Are you happy?"

"Yes."

"Me, too."

She looked at him carefully. "Is it wrong to feel this way when Lance is still missing?"

"We're doing everything possible to get him back."

"I know, but I still feel guilty."

"So do I, but that doesn't stop me from wanting you. Does that make me an insensitive s.o.b.?"

"No," she whispered. "It makes you human."

"Maybe, or maybe it's called living for the moment. I learned to do that in Nam, thinking that each breath I drew might be my last one. I swore on the spot that if I made it out of that hellhole, I wouldn't waste another second of my life."

"I sort of felt that way when Daddy was struck with Alzheimer's."

Without warning, he unhooked her top and thrust it aside. Together they watched it float away.

He turned back to her and for the longest time merely looked at her. "Do you know your skin glows in the moonlight?"

She smiled. "No." Her lashes fluttered; he brushed his mouth against them.

Then lowering his head, he ran his lips across her shoulders.

"Mmm, your mustache tickles," she mused aloud.

"Like it, huh?"

"Love it," she gasped as he took a soft bite from her shoulder. "I've never had the pleasure before... you."

He stopped what he was doing and chuckled. "Really?"

"Really, and it's dynamite against my skin," she whispered, wrapping her arms around his neck and returning the favor.

He moaned as her mouth made contact with his skin, hot and sweet.

"Marnie, Marnie, you make me crazy."

"Good."

He bent down and tongued a nipple. When she moaned deep in her throat, he lifted his head and watched her expression as he tongued the other nipple.

She dug her nails into his arms. He had to care. *He had to love her.* Surely it wasn't just sex. But because she was still riddled with doubt, she continued to hold on to her sanity and refused to be swept away by this hunger he created within her.

She inched her hands down and cupped the cheeks of his buttocks. They felt so hard, so smooth, so perfect.

"Does riding do this for you? Keep you in such good shape, I mean?"

"That and jogging." His mouth split into a grin. "I refuse to have a beer belly."

"I can't see that ever happening. You're too... perfect," she added shyly, feeling his hardness surge between them.

"But not nearly as perfect as you," he said, moving against her.

She couldn't speak.

His hands spanned her waist. "You're so tiny here."

"Exercise," she said breathlessly.

"What about here?" He laid his hands on her hips where he began to dislodge her trunks. "Is your tight little butt from exercise, too?" he asked, his fingers seeking and finding her warmth.

Suddenly her legs threatened to buckle beneath her. "I don't know," she whispered. "Please...oh... you're..."

"Wrap your legs around me," he ordered urgently, cupping her buttocks.

"Have you ever made love like this before?"

"No."

A warm sensation curled through her, but she couldn't tell him how he made her feel. And as he expanded inside her, all coherent thoughts fled her mind.

"Marnie," he whispered against her neck, "I don't want to hurt you."

"Let's get out, then," she said urgently, on fire for him.

Moments later found them on the grass where Tate immediately slipped into her. Then with her fingers sinking into his back, his lips dusted her neck, then danced down her stomach.

He pressed deeper into her. She reveled in his strength, hot and pulsing, as he began to move faster and faster. Her hands held him to her while he burst within her, almost stopping her breath. Then she exhaled in one long, shuddering sigh and dropped slowly back to earth.

The smell of bacon awakened her. She stretched, then smiled, remembering. With that smile still intact, Marnie reached out a hand to the space next to her. Empty. Tate was gone. Though disappointed, she wasn't surprised.

She glanced at the clock. Seven o'clock. He was probably already at the office. Since it was Annie who was responsible for the heavenly smell, Marnie made no effort to get up. She wanted to think.

Their lovemaking that began in the pool and ended in her bed had been more than perfect. She lay waiting for that delicious shiver of remembrance to rush through her. But this time it didn't come. Fear came instead. What was she going to do when she had to give him up?

A short time later, after having showered and slipped into a caftan, Marnie padded into the kitchen, only to pull up short.

"Tate?"

He spun around from in front of the stove and grinned. "Mornin'."

"Morning," she said, walking deeper into the room. She didn't stop until she was beside him. He looked so sexy in a pair of cutoff jeans and worn T-shirt that she almost melted on the spot. "Where's Annie?"

"She's off."

"Oh."

He laughed. "What does that mean? Don't you think I'm capable of fixing you something to eat?"

"Mmm," she teased. "We'll just have to wait and see.

He laid the fork down and pulled her against him.

Marnie angled her head so that she could see him. His lashes were damp and thick. "Why aren't you at work?"

"I will be shortly."

"You smell absolutely delicious," she said, inhaling deeply.

He nibbled on her neck. "Not nearly as good as you, and if you don't move your you-know-what to that chair, I'm going to haul your delectable body back to bed."

Weakly, Marnie moved out of his arms and sat down.

"Chicken."

She made a face. "Not chicken, just exhausted."

He threw back his head and laughed, then poured her a cup of coffee.

She had just taken the cup from him and sat down when the kitchen door opened. She peered beyond Tate's shoulder, only to feel the cup slip from her hand.

Lance! she mouthed.

"Hello, my darling Marnie."

Marnie blinked back the tears. Still they came, saturating her cheeks, dripping into her mouth. Frantically, she delved into her purse, yanked out a Kleenex and wiped her face. What was wrong with her? She should be laughing instead of crying. Lance was back. He had made an amazing escape. That was cause for celebration, not tears.

Self-flagellation did not help. She had existed under such a strain for so long that even though the crisis was over, her emotions couldn't cope.

Finally gaining some measure of control, Marnie stole a glance at Tate. They were the sole occupants of the waiting room at a small private hospital on Houston's west side. It was obvious that relief had also escaped him.

He was staring out the window, his face grim, his shoulders rigid. He had changed out of his cutoffs and was wearing jeans and a sports shirt. She longed to reach out to him, to comfort him, but he suddenly seemed untouchable.

She tried to tell herself that his aloofness was not directed toward her personally, that he was consumed with worry over Lance. Since their arrival at the hospital over two hours ago, the doctor hadn't let Tate see Lance, nor had the doctor come and talked to him.

Unable to handle the silence another minute, Marnie got up from the leather sofa and went to the coffee bar. Once there, she turned and faced Tate's back. "Would you like a cup of coffee?"

Tate swung around and leveled his gaze on her. For an instant she thought she saw his eyes soften, but she couldn't be sure.

"No thanks. I think I'd choke on it."

Suddenly Marnie lost her desire for any, as well. Still, coffee in her stomach, she reasoned, was better than nothing.

"Wonder what's taking them so long?" she asked, gripping the cup tightly.

"Beats me," Tate said, his tone clipped. "As far as I know, Dr. Mays hasn't even let the FBI in to see him."

"Well, thank Heavens he's alive," she mused aloud.

"Yeah," Tate muttered, "but just barely."

Marnie could understand Tate's impatience and concern. When Lance had walked into the kitchen, they had been speechless. But shock hadn't affected their eyesight. They had soaked up Lance's bruised and battered face. He looked as if he'd been in a boxing match and lost. Both cheeks were black and blue. A cut shone above his upper lip. And it had been apparent he hadn't eaten a decent meal since he'd been gone. He was skin and bones.

"Oh, Lance," Marnie had cried at last, forcing her jellylike legs to move in his direction.

"Lord, son," Tate said, closing the distance between them, as well.

Tate reached Lance first and embraced him. Marnie saw the tears in Tate's eyes and looked away, all the while grappling with her own torrid emotions.

Once Lance disentangled himself from Tate, he reached for Marnie. She went willingly into his arms and embraced his weakened body.

"Oh, Lance," she cried again, "thank God you're back."

"Thank God is right," Tate echoed. "There were times when I didn't think I'd see you again." He stopped for a moment and drew in a harsh breath.

"My feelings exactly," Lance said weakly. "But I finally outwitted those sonofabitches." He gently pushed Marnie away and looked at Tate. "It wasn't easy."

Tate's Adam's apple worked overtime. "No, I'm sure it wasn't," he responded in a tight voice.

There was a moment of emotion-filled silence, then Tate cleared his throat and asked, "Did the FBI stop you at the gate?"

Lance nodded. "An army of them, but I told 'em I wanted to surprise you. I think I need to sit down," Lance added, mopping his brow.

"What you need is the hospital. Now." Tate's eyes sought Marnie's. "Get the car and I'll help Lance."

Minutes later, with two FBI cars trailing behind, Tate maneuvered the car onto the highway. Lance was sprawled across the back seat while Marnie sat up front with Tate.

However, Marnie kept her gaze locked on Lance, fearing he might pass out before they reached their destination.

"Don't you want to hear what happened?" Lance asked in a strained voice.

Tate's eyes were reflected in the rearview mirror. "Only if you're up to it."

"I'm... all right," Lance said, his gaze encompassing Marnie, as well.

Marnie didn't believe him for a second, and she knew Tate didn't, either. Anyone as banged up as Lance couldn't be all right.

"All I want is for those bastards to pay," Lance added, his voice regaining some of its lost strength.

"Oh, they'll pay, all right." Tate's tone was sharp and menacing.

Marnie shivered.

"Did you miss me, darling?" Lance asked, intruding on her thoughts.

Color surged into Marnie's face, and she dared not look at Tate. "Of course I...we...did. I..." She couldn't go on; her voice broke.

"I'm glad," Lance said warmly.

"How the hell did you get away?" Tate's voice sounded suddenly disembodied.

"Most of the time the bastards were both there for meals, but early this morning only one came— Anderson. When he untied my hands and gave me the slop he called hot cereal, I threw it in his face and ran like hell."

A smile flirted with Tate's lips. "Did you give them a hard time?"

Marnie looked on as Lance tried to smile; it turned into a wince instead. "I wish. But I didn't have a chance. The minute they shoved me inside this dark hole they called a room, they both took turns using me as a punching bag."

Marnie grieved for Lance. "Oh, God, they sound like animals."

"Worse," Tate said in a cold, flat voice.

"I heard them talking. They planned to hold you up for a ton of money," Lance said, sounding drained to the bottom.

Marnie had wondered when he was going to come off his adrenaline high. It had taken longer than she had thought.

"That's what we figured," Tate said, "ruling out that your abduction had nothing to do with the explosives project. But what we couldn't figure is why they waited so long to make their demands."

"Because the longer they held me, the more anxious you'd become."

A frown slashed Tate's face. "And give 'em what they asked for without quibbling?"

"That's right. Elliot was the brains behind the whole thing," Lance said, his voice once again beginning to fade. "After he was fired, he talked his good buddy Anderson into helping him."

Muscles bunched in Tate's shoulders. "It's a damn wonder they pulled it off. There's not enough brains between the two of them to fill a thimble."

"That's the sweet truth," Lance said, closing his eyes.

While Lance slept, Tate had concentrated on getting them safely to the hospital. Now, as they waited for the doctor, his patience was wearing thin.

"Are you sure you don't want some coffee?" Marnie asked again, sipping on hers. "It tastes really good."

Tate stared at her in brooding silence for a moment, then said, "Positive."

"What about your mother?" Marnie spoke quickly. Anything, she told herself, was better than the clawing tension between them. "Do...you want me to call her?"

"I'll do it, but thanks anyway." Tate's features relented somewhat. "Only I want to wait until Dr. Mays comes and talks to us."

As if on cue, the doctor strode into the room, a grin adding relief to his harsh face and lips.

"It's good news, Tate. Physically Lance is going to be just fine. There are no internal injuries."

Tate seemed to wilt. "That's damn good news."

"What about mentally?" Marnie put in anxiously, taking things a step further.

Dr. Mays's features changed. "Now that's a different matter altogether."

"What does that mean?" Tate asked sharply, his eyes narrowing.

"Calm down, Tate. Don't go gettin' your dander up. Your boy's been through hell and it's going to take time. I'm..."

"Spit it out, Clay."

"All right," Dr. Mays said, fixing his gaze on Tate. "There will more than likely be mental repercussions."

Tate's expression tightened. "So what do you suggest?"

Marnie's heart went out to him, and again she ached to touch him, to comfort him. Still she did neither. She simply ached in silence.

"I suggest that he remain here in the hospital for a few days under a psychiatrist's care."

"Whatever it takes." Tate's tone was dull.

There was a short silence.

"Can we see him?" Tate finally asked, his eyes on Marnie.

Dr. Mays didn't hesitate. "No problem."

"What about the FBI?"

"No problem there, either."

When they walked into Lance's stark room a few minutes later, Lance was prone on the bed, a frown on his face. He no longer looked as weak and washed out as he had earlier. In addition, he seemed to have regained some of his confidence.

"When can I go home?" His tone now had a sullen edge to it.

Relief shot through Marnie. Flashes of the old Lance—arrogant and spoiled to be exact—meant he was rebounding. However, she didn't think Tate shared her view.

"Not for a few days, I'm afraid," Tate said, crossing to Lance's bedside. "The doctor wants to keep you here for observation."

"Why?" Lance demanded. "I'm fine."

Tate flashed Marnie a brief glance, then turned back to his son.

"No, you're *not* fine."

"Well, the only way I'll stay is if Marnie stays with me."

Thrown into sudden confusion, Marnie couldn't say a word.

"Marnie?" Lance said again, a petulant ring to his voice.

Swallowing a sigh, Marnie crossed to the other side of the bed and placed her hand in his. "I'll be here as much as I can," she whispered, knowing her voice sounded unlike her own. Dear Lord, she was trying. But with Tate watching...

"It—it was thoughts of you that kept me sane." Lance paused and tightened his grip on her hand. "You won't leave me now, will you?"

The sudden stillness in the room was like a deafening roar.

Marnie lifted her head and met Tate's eyes, eyes that were as empty and bleak as a harsh winter day. Then he looked away.

Trying to ignore the stabbing pain around her heart, she forced herself to say, "No, I won't leave you."

Marnie remained true to her word. Almost every spare moment of every day was spent with Lance. It was only in the evenings that she returned to the ranch. And without fail found Tate absent.

She had wanted to go back to her condo, but until the kidnappers were apprehended, neither Tate nor the FBI thought that was a good idea.

During that week the blissful times she and Tate had spent in each other's arms seemed more a dream than a reality. His odd behavior not only puzzled her, but upset her, as well.

Was it guilt that kept him from coming to her, or something else? It was that "something else" that had her nearly crazy.

The situation with Lance was a delicate one, she knew, and must be handled with care and caution. But just because it was impossible to blurt the truth to Lance right now shouldn't mean that she and Tate couldn't be together.

Instead of looking on the dark side, Marnie clung to the hope that once Lance got out of the hospital, things would return to normal—Tate would return to normal. What then? Would they tell Lance they were lovers? Yes. She was willing. But she honestly didn't know how Tate felt. The uncertainty was tearing her to pieces.

In the meantime she kept her promise to Lance, though each day was more trying than the one before. Lance's personality had undergone another change, a change that was definitely unpleasant. One would think that his ordeal would have matured him, made him look at life differently. Not so. If anything, Lance seemed more self-centered, more demanding than ever.

He was responding to treatment, even though at times he was plagued by nightmares and periods of deep depression. The majority of the time, it was all Marnie could do not to shake him.

Since she'd arrived at his room two hours ago, he'd been griping about everything in general and nothing in particular.

From her chair close to the bed, Marnie said, "I've decided nothing is wrong with you other than you're spoiled."

Lance gave her a dark look. "You've been around my father too much."

She took a deep breath to ease the pressure within her.

"What's with you two, anyway?"

Ignoring his question and determined to steer the conversation onto a safe subject, Marnie said, "I keep thinking Dr. Mays is going to release you."

"Yeah, me too. The food stinks."

Marnie rolled her eyes. "Surely that's not the only reason you're anxious to leave?"

Lance reached for her hand and began caressing it. "No," he said, his voice low. "The main reason is that I want to make love to you."

"Lance, please," Marnie said between clenched teeth, wanting to scream in frustration. "We've—"

"Am I interrupting anything?"

Feeling her heart sink to her toes, Marnie forced herself to turn toward the door. Tate was leaning nonchalantly against the frame, looking cool and unflappable. Marnie sensed his mood was anything but. He refused to meet her eyes.

"Come in," she finally said, removing her hand from Lance's grasp. "You're . . . not interrupting anything."

"Says who?" Lance put in, a belligerent slant to his lips.

"Sorry," Tate said, only he didn't sound sorry. He sounded furious, Marnie thought. His nostrils were flaring.

When he spoke, his voice was calm, though a bit rough. "I've got some good news."

Marnie didn't say anything. Nevertheless, he had her full attention. He looked wonderful, and she yearned to touch him.

"Anderson and Elliot have been arrested," he said.

"'Bout time," Lance said.

"I second that," Marnie added, still trying to get Tate to look at her, but without success. He seemed more than ever bent on ignoring her, and each time he did, she died a little on the inside.

"Does that mean they'll go straight to the pen?" Lance was asking.

"If I have my way, the bastards will fry."

"Or at least stay locked up for the rest of their lives," Marnie added.

Tate's gaze rested on her. In that second something trembled between them.

"You're out of danger now, you know." Tate's voice was thin.

"That . . . means I can go home."

"That's right." Tate drew a ragged breath. "That ought to make you happy."

What about you? Marnie wanted to scream. *Does it make you happy?* "It does, of course," she murmured politely, as if she were discussing the weather with a complete stranger.

If Lance sensed the tension in the room, he chose to ignore it. "Well, it makes me happy. It makes me damn happy."

Neither Marnie nor Tate said a word.

Again their silence seemed not to bother Lance. He went on, though he only had eyes for Marnie. "Maybe now I can convince you to marry me."

The air was fraught with tension.

Marnie's eyes swung to Tate; hers were pleading. A white line surrounded his lips.

"You two don't need me." Tate's voice was flat. "I'll see you later."

With that he walked out the door. Marnie sat in pained silence, feeling as if he'd taken part of her heart with him.

"Is that all, boss?"

"Yeah, Neal. I think that about does it for now."

"Good. I'll see to these contracts, then."

The instant Tate was alone, he got up, strode to the bar and poured himself a drink. Hell, he knew it was too early in the day to be indulging, but he didn't give a damn.

He had to have something to dull the pain.

He knew it would happen. And it had. She was breaking his goddamn heart, and there was nothing he could do about it.

He should have known better than to get involved with her. Dammit, he should never have touched her to begin with.

It was too late for self-recriminations. All there was to do now was suffer. Every time he saw her and Lance together, it was as though someone jammed a knife into his heart. It was worst when Lance touched her.

He had no right to feel that way. Marnie didn't belong with him. Not only was he too old for her, but too jaded. Sure, he could give her material things—the best money could buy. But that wasn't enough. In the end he knew that wouldn't hold her. Even money, after so long a time, paled.

No, she deserved someone better. She deserved someone young, someone who could make her laugh, fill a house with children's laughter.

But was that someone his son? In the beginning he'd been against a relationship between them, for all the wrong reasons. He'd thought Marnie was a gold digger and he'd felt Lance was too spoiled and selfish for a lasting relationship. But now he truly believed that Lance was in love. And if he, Tate, stepped out of the picture, Marnie would find happiness with Lance, as it should be.

Suddenly a bitter taste flooded Tate's mouth and he had the urge to throw the glass in his hand against the wall. Suddenly he did just that, the sound rocking the room like a small explosion. When quiet finally came, he felt no better.

Completely drained, he sat down and slumped over his desk, head in his hands.

How was he ever going to let her go? He didn't know. He honestly didn't know.

"Tate...I want to talk to you. Please."

Marnie, as she'd done once before, had decided to wait up for him, no matter how late the hour. This was her last night at the ranch; tomorrow she planned to return to her condo.

Before she left, though, she had to get some answers from Tate. If it was over between them, she wanted him to say it. If he didn't want to ever hold her again or make love to her again, she wanted him to tell her to her face.

Lance's two-week stint in the hospital was coming to an end. He was due to be released in a few more days. During that second week, Tate had remained his unapproachable self. She simply couldn't take it anymore.

Away from Tate, her life had ceased to have meaning. Things that had been important to her paled in comparison to her feelings for Tate.

Now, as she confronted him at eleven o'clock in the evening, she wasn't sure her idea was a good one, after all. If his foreboding features were anything by which to judge, he wasn't thrilled to see her.

"What about?" he asked, treading lightly into the room, then tossing his briefcase on the bar, where he mixed himself a drink.

Marnie nursed her lower lip. She had rehearsed this speech over and over, only to feel the words suddenly desert her along with her nerve. Finally she forced them out.

"You know what about. Us."

With his free hand Tate yanked at the tie around his neck. "There's no us, Marnie," he said flatly. "There never was."

She felt as if he'd speared her heart. "But—"

"Does Lance still want to marry you?"

"Yes, but—"

"Good. You have my blessings."

Ten

Marnie went pale, and the floor underneath her feet seemed to shift. He wanted her to marry Lance. *Impossible!* He didn't mean that. He *couldn't* mean that.

"What—what did you say?" Even to her own ears, her voice sounded as if she were dying.

Tate shoved a hand through his hair. "You heard me," he said tersely.

"But I don't understand...." Marnie shook her head in misery and bewilderment. There had always been that deep-seated fear that he didn't love her, after all. Still, she hadn't dreamed their relationship would end like this. Oh, God, not like this. "You—you can't mean that," she wheezed.

"I mean it," he said, his voice sounding hollow.

Marnie flinched visibly. This wasn't the same man who so recently had taken her in his arms and made love to her, deeply and passionately. This was a cold, hard stranger whom she barely recognized.

"You had to know it would end sometime," he said, his eyes never leaving her face.

Marnie refused to let him know how much he was hurting her. She lifted her chin, though it shook despite her efforts to the contrary. "Are you doing this because you think I'm not good enough for you?"

"Hell!" His disgust was obvious. "If I thought that, would I be encouraging you to marry my son?"

Marnie caught her breath and worked on ignoring the lump stuck in her throat. "I don't want to marry Lance. I've never wanted to marry Lance. He's...a spoiled rich kid who's never grown up." She paused, trembling. "Is it because Lance touched me and I didn't pull away...?"

"Look, let me make it clear right now that it's not jealousy that's causing me to end our relationship." He paused and breathed deeply. "Although, I will admit, it nearly ripped my gut to pieces."

"Oh, Tate," Marnie whimpered.

"But at the same time," he went on, as if she hadn't spoken, "I saw how right you two were together, how much happier he could make you than I."

"That's not true!"

"Face it, Marnie, I'm too old for you."

"That's ridiculous," she cried, twisting her fingers together. "Age doesn't matter when you love someone," she added, brokenhearted.

"What about children?"

"What about them?"

He snorted. "You deserve to have them, and I'm too old to start over."

"That's simple. We won't have any. Anyway, I want you, not children.'"

"You say that now," he said stubbornly.

She placed her hands over her ears. "Stop it! Stop it right now! Stop trying to put the blame on me. It's you who's making the excuses." She choked on a sob. "You're the one who's afraid, who can't make the commitment, who—who doesn't love me!"

"Dammit, that's not it!"

"Then what is it?" She was begging now, but she didn't care. "Lance? Is that it? Is that what this is all about? Guilt?"

Looking at him, into his smoldering eyes, she felt her senses stir with a primitive emotion only he could arouse in her.

"It's over, Marnie." He swallowed hard. "There's no other way."

"Oh, Tate," she breathed. "Don't make this the end, please. Sacrificing us for Lance won't work. He's not for me. Can't you see that?"

Tate's eyes were filled with agony. "Do you think I wanted it this way?" he muttered harshly.

She deliberately moved closer to him, aching to smell him, touch him, wrap her arms around his flesh.

"Oh, God, Marnie," he groaned. Then pulling her to him, he parted her lips with his own.

Fiercely, she clung. Coherent thoughts refused to form, words refused to come. Only the urgency of wordless, pristine need sustained her.

Then it was over. His breath ragged, Tate thrust her away and turned, his shoulders bent as if from an unbearable weight.

Tears streaked Marnie's cheeks. Oh, God, she was losing the battle. His guilt was proving too powerful a stumbling block to overcome.

"Tate..."

"Don't...Marnie." His voice sounded strangled. "It's over."

Suddenly desperate, Marnie grabbed his arm and spun him around. "Tell me you don't love me!" she cried. "Look me in the eye and tell me that."

Tate hesitated, looking as if there was nothing left inside him. But when he spoke, his tone was low and even. "I don't love you."

There was so much she wanted to say, so much she wanted to do. But she did nothing. Instead, she just stood there and watched as he turned and walked out the door.

With a muted cry she sank to her knees, harsh sobs racking her body.

Tate's cruel rejection of her had been a blow to her heart. Only her pride saw her through the dark week that followed.

She had avoided Tate, which hadn't been difficult as things at the office were under control, leaving him free to remain at the ranch.

While he'd gone on a horse-buying trip, she'd quickly and quietly moved out of the ranch and back into her condo. Kate's presence had been a godsend.

"I'd like to give that bastard a piece of my mind," she'd said as soon as Marnie filled her in on the latest developments.

Just thinking about Kate's flashing eyes and wrinkled nose brought a fleeting smile to Marnie's lips.

"Marnie."

Shaking her head and forcing herself back to the moment at hand, she turned around and faced Lance. Because of a minor setback, he hadn't been released from the hospital.

"Yes," she said, smiling at him absently.

"We've spent a lot of time together lately, right?"

"Yes," she said again, her tone guarded.

"So doesn't that prove that we'd make a great team—"

She waved her hand in silent protest. "Don't, Lance. Don't even start. I know where you're headed, and it won't work. Anyway, you promised that the word *us* would not be discussed."

Red washed Lance's face. "Dammit, Marnie, I'm not going to give you up without a fight."

She bounded out of the chair. "You have no choice," she said coldly. "The sooner you understand that, the sooner you can get on with your life."

There was a long pause, which solved nothing.

"Is he good in bed?"

Marnie's eyes widened in astonishment.

"Gawd." Lance drawled out the word. "Don't play the innocent with me."

"Lance..."

"I know about you and my father."

Marnie felt her stomach drop away. "How...long have you known?"

"I might have had a few licks on the head, but I'm not blind, Marnie." His tone was cutting.

She straightened. "I never thought you were."

"So when's the wedding?"

"There's...not going to be—" her voice cracked "—a wedding."

"So he won't marry you, huh?"

Hot, boiling fury coursed through her. "Go to hell, Lance."

He laughed darkly. "Most likely I will, thanks to you."

Marnie gasped.

As if sensing he had gone too far, he said, "Look—"

Marnie cut him off tersely. "I'm going to quit the company, so you won't have to worry about me being around." She paused and with forced steadiness walked to the door. "Then, I'll probably leave town."

"Does Tate know?"

"No, and I'm not going to tell him, either." She paused and raised a hand to her heart; she could feel the thunder of its beat. "I guess this is goodbye, Lance."

Lance stood at the edge of the bed and jammed his hands into the pockets of his jeans. "If you walk out that door, you'll be making a mistake."

She turned the knob.

"Dammit, I'm every bit the man my father is!"

Marnie spun around, her eyes flashing. "Grow up, Lance. You'll never be the man Tate is."

When she walked down the hall a second later, she could still see Lance's gaping mouth.

For the first time in a long while, Marnie smiled from the heart.

Tate knew he would pay for rebuilding the entire fence on the south side of the pasture at one whack. But he didn't care. Manual labor had once again saved his sanity.

J.D., his beer belly wiggling like a bowl of jelly, had all but threatened to quit if Tate didn't stop working so hard. Tate had just as quickly told him that he'd do what he damned well pleased on his own ranch.

Muttering something under his breath, J.D. had stamped off. Then he'd stopped, wheeled around and said, "Whatever's got you all torn up inside is gonna cause you to break your back."

Now, as Tate dropped his hammer and stood, the sun bearing down on him with no mercy, he admitted that J.D. had been right. He didn't know how much longer he would be able to survive without Marnie. No amount of physical abuse had been able to drive her from his heart.

Was she right? Was he just using guilt as an excuse when in reality he was a coward? Was he afraid to take a chance on love again? Afraid to make a commitment? Or was the reason more pointed than that? Was he afraid to love *Marnie*, for fear she would soon tire of him? She was so young, so full of life.

And, ultimately, was he strong enough, unselfish enough, to let her marry Lance? Just the thought of them making love... well, he couldn't bear to think about that.

Yet that was a real possibility. After all, he'd more than done his part to bring it about. Still, Lance had not mentioned Marnie since he'd been home, and Tate hadn't asked.

Tears burned his eyes. He raised an unsteady hand, covering them. The sunlight seemed to pierce his brain. He fought for breath.

Suddenly the sound of horse's hooves claimed his attention. Once again shading his eyes, he peered into the distance and watched a rider approach. It was Lance.

Swallowing a tired sigh, Tate made his way toward his son. Momentarily, he grasped the mare's reins and peered up into Lance's face. "What's up?"

Without preamble Lance said, "I need to talk to you."

"Sure thing." Tate removed his Stetson and wiped his brow. "Only not here in this sun."

Silently, Lance and horse followed Tate to a huge oak that provided more than ample shade. Tate propped himself against it while Lance rested an elbow on the saddle.

"Is something wrong?" Tate asked at last, a fear of another kind festering inside him.

"I'm moving out, getting an apartment."

"You won't get any argument out of me," Tate said easily. "It's past time you were on your own."

"Marnie's leaving."

If it was his intent to shock, Lance had hit the mark. Tate went still; every nerve in his body seemed to stop functioning. "Leaving?"

"Yeah, as in the company." Lance's tone now held a note of triumph, as though taking great delight in telling Tate that. "Maybe even Houston."

Refusing to rise to the bait, though his insides were clamoring, Tate forced his expression to remain blank. "I'm . . . that's too bad."

Lance snorted. "Hell, Dad, spare me the rhetoric. I know about you and Marnie."

Tate suddenly felt cold inside. "There is no Marnie and me. I won't stand in your way if you still want to marry her."

"And take your leftovers? No thanks."

Blood thundered to Tate's head and his eyes iced over. "I ought to make you apologize for that remark—or better still, I ought to drag you off that horse and beat the daylights out of you."

When Lance didn't say anything, Tate hammered on, "I thought that Marnie would be better off with you, but I was wrong. Dead wrong. I love you son, but

God help me, I've ruined you. And until you grow up, you're of no use to anyone, most of all yourself.''

Lance eased off the saddle onto the ground where he pawed the grass. "Look, I'm sorry, I was way out of line—''

"You damn straight you were."

"About you . . . and Marnie—''

"That's no longer any of your damn business."

Lance turned red, but when he spoke, his voice was forceful. "Well, just for the record, I think you're a fool if you let her go."

"I couldn't agree more."

"So now can we talk, really talk?"

"Later," Tate said, spinning around and heading for his mount, which was grazing close by.

"Where you going?"

Tate didn't miss a stride. "Guess."

"Are you sure quitting your job is for the best?"

Marnie stared at Kate and smiled bleakly. "No, right now I'm not sure of anything, other than the fact that I can't continue working for Tate and keep my sanity."

They were in Marnie's condo, sitting on the couch and drinking coffee. Both their expressions were sober, as sober as the weather outside. Rain was falling. The night was warm.

"Boy, did that bastard do a number on you."

"That he did," Marnie agreed on a shaky note. "This sounds crazy, I know, but the only time I find peace of mind is when I visit Daddy."

"Have you told Tate yet?" Kate asked after a moment.

"I told Lance instead."

"So what happens now?"

"I'm—I'm going to look for another job."

"Oh, Marnie, honey, I wish I could say something, anything that would make you stop hurting."

Marnie felt numb, but she had to handle it. "Me, too, only we both know that's impossible."

Kate opened her mouth to respond only to be cut off by the chiming of the doorbell. "You expecting company?"

Through unwanted tears, Marnie peered at the clock on the wall. "Not at ten o'clock."

"Want me to answer it?"

"Please," Marnie whispered, drawing the sash on her paisley robe tighter and struggling to regain her composure. Every time she thought about Tate, talked about him, she cried. Just getting through each day was hell.

"Marnie."

She could tell by the tone of Kate's voice that something was wrong. With her heart in her throat, Marnie swung around.

Tate stood in the shadows of the entrance hall, his eyes fixed on her. For a moment Marnie couldn't function, could hardly breathe.

His hair and mustache sparkled with raindrops under the muted lamplight. His jeans and blue shirt were wet, as well, adhering to his body like a second skin.

No one spoke; the silence was long and heavy.

Then Kate coughed and stammered, "M-Marnie, hon, I gotta run. I'll...talk to you later."

Marnie could only nod and watch as Kate scooted out the door.

Still Marnie did not move, nor did Tate. They could only stare, their eyes devouring each other.

"God, Marnie, I've..."

Marnie steeled her heart against his husky tone and the agony in his eyes. "What are you doing here?" she whispered, barely able to stem the tide of her emotions. He looked so big, so strong, so dear....

"Lance told me you were leaving."

"He shouldn't have."

Tate smiled at that, only it never reached his eyes. "Did you think I wouldn't find out?"

She didn't answer.

"That's not all he told me."

"Oh." her voice was faint.

"He told me I was a fool."

Her eyes widened.

"Yeah, imagine that," Tate said with a cynical smile. "Imagine my son telling me I was a fool and my agreeing with him."

Marnie couldn't remove her gaze, held spellbound by what he was saying.

Her voice trembled. "I . . . don't know why you came, but it's late and—"

"I love you, Marnie."

For a second she thought her ears were playing tricks on her. Or was she hearing words that she had only heard echoing in the chambers of her heart?

When she didn't respond, Tate edged closer. "I love you," he said again, his voice warm, colored with passion.

Stifling a cry, Marnie reached for him, her eyes brimming with tears. When he crushed her against him, she felt his strength surge through her. "Tate. Oh, Tate . . . I missed you so. I love you." She didn't want to hold back or hide anything from him.

"Can you ever forgive me?" he asked desperately. "You were right about everything. I was afraid. But once a dream is shattered, trust comes hard."

Marnie pulled back. "What—what about Lance?" She had to ask. She had to know.

Tate bracketed her face with his hands and looked into her eyes. "I tried to do what I thought was best for him, for you, only it wasn't." He paused as if struggling to get the words out. "I love him, but God help me, I love you more."

The sounds of belonging rang in his tearful whisper. The firm strength of his arms was tender and gentle.

"Don't," she whispered, opening her lips to his. They kissed, hotly and deeply, their mouths speaking their hearts' desires.

"Oh, Marnie," Tate whispered, clutching her tightly, their tears mingling. "Marry me. Now."

Something eased within Marnie's heart while they seemed suspended in time.

"Hold me, Tate. Don't ever let me go."

"Never, my darling, never."

* * * * *

SILHOUETTE® *Desire*™

COMING NEXT MONTH

#577 CANDLELIGHT FOR TWO—Annette Broadrick
Steve Donovan was the last person Jessica Sheldon wanted to accompany
her to Australia. Can two people who've made fighting into an art find
forever in each other's arms?

#578 NOT EASY—Lass Small
Detective Winslow Homer thought finding Penelope Rutherford's missing
camera would be a snap. But it wasn't so easy—and neither was getting
Penelope to admit that she found him irresistible!

#579 ECHOES FROM THE HEART—Kelly Jamison
Brenna McShane had never forgotten her very sexy—and very
unreliable—ex-husband. Then Luke McShane returned, bringing
home all the remembered pain . . . and all the remembered passion of
their young love.

#580 YANKEE LOVER—Beverly Barton
Historian Laurel Drew was writing her ancestor's biography when
unrefined John Mason showed up with a different story. Soon sparks were
flying between this Southern belle and her Yankee lover.

#581 BETWEEN FRIENDS—Candace Spencer
When reasonable Logan Fletcher proposed marriage to his best friend,
Catherine Parrish, it wasn't for love. Could he ever understand
Catherine's utterly romantic reasons for accepting?

#582 HOTSHOT—Kathleen Korbel
July's *Man of the Month*, photojournalist Devon Kane liked to be where
the action was. But with his latest subject—reclusive Libby Matthews—
Devon found the greatest adventure was love!

AVAILABLE NOW:

#571 SLOW BURN
Mary Lynn Baxter

#572 LOOK BEYOND THE DREAM
Noelle Berry McCue

#573 TEMPORARY HONEYMOON
Katherine Granger

#574 HOT ON HER TRAIL
Jean Barrett

#575 SMILES
Cathie Linz

#576 SHOWDOWN
Nancy Martin

Silhouette Intimate Moments®

**Beginning this month, Intimate Moments brings
you the first of two gripping stories by Emilie Richards**

Coming in June
Runaway
by EMILIE RICHARDS
Intimate Moments #337

Coming in July
The Way Back Home
by EMILIE RICHARDS
Intimate Moments #341

Krista and Rosie Jensen were two sisters who had it all—until a
painful secret tore them apart.

They were two special women who met two very special men who
made life a little easier—and love a whole lot better—until the day
when Krista and Rosie could be sisters once again.

You'll laugh, you'll cry and you'll never, ever forget. RUNAWAY is
available now at your favorite retail outlet, or order your copy by
sending your name, address, zip or postal code along with a check
or money order for $2.95, plus 75¢ postage and handling, payable
to Silhouette Reader Service to:

In the U.S.	In Canada
901 Fuhrmann Blvd.	P.O. Box 609
Box 1396	Fort Erie, Ontario
Buffalo, NY 14269-1396	L2A 5X3

Please specify book title with your order.

Silhouette Books®

RUN-1A

Silhouette Romance®

CIMARRON STORIES

A TRILOGY BY PEPPER ADAMS

Pepper Adams is back and spicier than ever with three tender, heartwarming tales, set on the plains of Oklahoma.

CIMARRON KNIGHT... available in June
Rugged rancher and dyed-in-the-wool bachelor Brody Sawyer meets his match in determined Noelle Chandler and her adorable twin boys!

CIMARRON GLORY... available in August
With a stubborn streak as strong as her foster brother Brody's, Glory Roberts has her heart set on lassoing handsome loner Ross Forbes... and uncovering his mysterious past....

CIMARRON REBEL... available in October
Brody's brother Riley is a handsome rebel with a cause! And he doesn't mind getting roped into marrying Darcy Durant—in name only—to gain custody of two heartbroken kids.

Don't miss CIMARRON KNIGHT, CIMARRON GLORY and CIMARRON REBEL—three special stories that'll win your heart... available only from Silhouette Romance!